GHOSTS
OF
BELLE ISLE

By Steven K. Smith

For more information, contact us at:

MyBoys3 Press, P.O. Box 2555, Midlothian, VA 23113

www.myboys3.com

Fourth Printing, 2020

ISBN: 978-0-9893414-8-6

To Mom and Dad,
For sending me downstream with a paddle in my boat

GHOSTS
OF
BELLE ISLE

AUTHOR'S NOTE

JULY, 2020

My family moved south to the Richmond area from New Jersey in the spring of 2011. As a "northern Yankee," I was quickly amazed and inspired by the history that burst from every corner, and I began imagining how to write exciting stories for young readers that featured historical themes. When I wrote *Ghosts of Belle Isle* in the summer of 2014, my view of the Civil War, segregation, and many issues that had been simmering in Virginia for generations was admittedly distant. I'd seen enough Confederate flags still flying to know that writing on themes tied to the Civil War could be complicated, so I attempted to tread lightly, speaking plainly to the evils of slavery, while seeking sensitivity to a southern culture that I was still working to understand.

The "grand" statues that lined Richmond's Monument Avenue didn't immediately strike me as hurtful or offensive objects, but rather unique artifacts from a different era whose chapter had been firmly closed by a Union victory. The suggestion of adding historical context and educational signage to the monuments seemed reasonable. I was surprised to learn that the comparatively small and understated statue of Abraham Lincoln behind Tredegar had faced significant opposition when it was unveiled in 2003.

Ghosts features three young kids who find themselves embroiled in an adventure that includes school bullies, mysterious legends of long-dead soldiers battling over the James River, a biker gang with southern pride and nostalgia for Confederate leaders like Jefferson Davis and Robert E. Lee, and other aspects from the war that ripped our young nation apart. As in life, some of the characters in this book are flawed—they can act kindly to children while also holding attitudes that might advance segrega-tionist and racist views. My goal was to prompt young readers (and perhaps older ones too) to question what brought us here, how they see the ever-changing world around them, and consider ways they might impact the future.

Remaining uneducated about a topic is often the easiest way to "innocently" ignore injustice. I'm now more intentionally listening to books and stories from voices whose experiences have differed widely from mine. These efforts are by no means complete, but as I've dug into the challenging history of reconstruction, Jim Crow, Massive Resistance, land annexation, and more, it's become clear that some things haven't changed as much as I'd assumed. While Richmond's monuments may have been erected to "glorify the southern cause," they also served to proclaim a stubborn determination to continue treating some people as less-than. Despite Jefferson's declaring that "all men are created equal," and Lincoln's formal proclamations of emancipation, Martin Luther King's dream of all people being treated equally has not been fulfilled.

Last week I walked back down Monument Avenue with my son on a hot Friday afternoon. I wanted to see with my own eyes the new reality of the Robert E. Lee statue, now blanketed in paint, emotional messages and banners, and small memorials with pictures of victims of racial violence. For many, the shadows cast by these enormous statues served as one of the barriers to true racial healing and reconciliation. The governor has stated plans to soon remove the sixty-foot bronze statue of General Lee from this spot, where he has towered above the avenue on horseback since 1890. Several of Richmond's Confederate statues have already come down, some upended from their hundred-year-old pedestals by the ropes of protestors, and others by city workers and cranes. To be sure, simply removing some statues will not build better schools, ensure more just treatment by the law, or bring greater economic opportunity, but it could be a start.

Six years have passed since I published *Ghosts*. That doesn't seem like a long time, yet the world feels different. I pray that amidst whatever turmoil still lies ahead, our land of imperfect people might come together to find ways to love, understand, and respect one another. That we might continue to strive for a more perfect union where all people are treated equally as they pursue life, liberty, and happiness. Thanks for reading.

CHAPTER ONE

It was three balls and two strikes in the bottom of the ninth of the backyard baseball game. Derek dug in at the plate, gripping the handle of his bat tightly. Sam ignored his brother's confident stare and stood tall on the flat stone that served as a pitching mound. He turned the ball in his hand behind his back so he could feel the laces. Slowly, his hands came together in front of his chest. He reared back, summoning his strength and focus. As he hurled his best heater toward the plate, he could almost hear the ball cutting through the air to the bottom right corner of the strike zone.

Derek waited patiently at the plate, hands at his ear, coiled like a snake about to strike. He swung in an instant, head down, watching the ball smack his bat as it flew through the zone. The ball shot off of his bat like a comet, flying higher and higher into the afternoon sky. It went over the big maple tree, over the fence that separated their yard from Old Man Haskins', and out of sight.

"Woohoo! Home run!" Derek shouted, jogging around the bases in exaggerated fashion with his arms raised over his head. "The Yankees win, theeeee Yankees win!" He dragged out the word *the* like the sports announcer on the radio up north was famous for doing.

Sam shook his head from the mound in the center of their backyard. He looked out to where the ball had disappeared. "Lucky shot, Derek. But now you've lost the ball."

"Lucky shot? Are you kidding?" said Derek, grinning. "That was pure skill. I crushed it! I'll bet that would have been over the fence at the little league field. Maybe the high school field. Maybe even Yankee Stadium!"

"Keep dreaming," Sam replied, draping a leg over the top board of the fence. He'd let Derek celebrate his moment of glory this time. The truth was, his older brother was a pretty good hitter. But Sam had been practicing his pitching for weeks against the bounce-back net their dad had bought him, and he felt like he was getting better. He silently vowed to strike Derek out next time.

"Where are you going?" called Derek. "Can't you handle the defeat?"

"I'm getting the ball!" said Sam scanning the neighboring yard from the top of the fence. He spied the ball underneath the pink flowers of a rhododendron bush and jumped down into a clump of old, dusty mulch, trying not to step on some flowers.

"Hey, that's trespassing you know, buster!" a gruff voice called through the trees.

Sam peered up from the shadows, picking out his neighbor along the side of the house. "Hey, Mr. Haskins," said Sam, warily. Mr. Haskins was eighty years old and a little kooky. Sam used to be afraid of him when his family moved to Virginia several years ago, but the old man was okay once you got to know him. "Sorry, I'm just getting our baseball."

"Baseball, huh? You're lucky you didn't break my windowpane, boy. I'd take that out of your allowance, if you have one. I'm not sure kids your age actually do any work anymore …"

Mr. Haskins was always harping on about how kids these days just sat inside and played video games. Sam slid off the fence and picked up the ball. He hesitated, contemplating just going back the way he had come, but then decided to be friendly and walked farther into the yard.

Mr. Haskins was wandering around the lawn in his bathrobe. It was white with long blue stripes running from top to bottom. He looked like he'd escaped from the county jail, or perhaps the local mental institution. Thankfully, he had clothes on underneath, as the robe hung open, its loose belt dragging in the grass. He wore an old, gray hat on his head and was muttering to himself.

"Isn't it time yet for school to start?" He peered over at Sam. "We need to get you back there before you break something."

Sam frowned. "It's only July, Mr. Haskins. We've still got half the summer left!" It seemed like summer was moving fast enough. He didn't want to wish it away sooner than he had to.

"Confounded dandelions!" the old man suddenly shouted.

Sam jumped at the noise. "What's the matter?"

"What's the matter?" Mr. Haskins repeated. "Look around! What do you see?"

"Grass?"

"Humph! Not much of it. Look at all those weeds. It's like I'm swimming in a sea of yellow out here. They're taking over, I tell ya!"

Sam looked around not knowing what to say. Mr. Haskins always seemed to be spouting off about something. It usually had to do with the weather or the mailman. "Maybe you need some fertilizer?" Sam thought he remembered hearing his dad say something about fertilizer being good for their yard.

"Fertilizer! Ha! That's the last thing I need, boy."

"Oh. Sorry." Apparently, that was the wrong answer.

"Fertilizer would just feed the weeds. I'm not wasting any of my hard-earned scratch just to feed those nasty buggers." His eyes grew large as he rambled on. "I've been thinking about—a master plan."

"A master plan?" asked Sam, raising his eyebrows. "You mean to get rid of the weeds?"

"No, a master plan to make you taller," yelled Mr. Haskins, smacking his forehead with his hand.

Sam tilted his head, trying to follow what the man was saying.

"Yes, I mean the weeds, boy. What do you think we're talking about here? Pay attention!" He turned back to the yard. "I'm thinking of setting the whole lawn on fire— one giant fireball would wipe 'em out once and for all!" Mr. Haskins raised his arms over his head in a dramatic motion like an atomic bomb exploding. "How do you think they'd like that?"

Sam took a cautious step back toward his house as he pictured Mr. Haskins' yard engulfed in flames. Maybe the old man had really lost it this time.

"That would be awesome!" exclaimed Derek, walking up behind them with a look of wonder on his face. "Can we help you?"

"Aww," muttered Mr. Haskins, waving off the boys with his hand. "Of course you kids would enjoy that, wouldn't you? I'm surprised you savages haven't set my place on fire already. Nah, I'm not going to give you or those weeds the satisfaction." He backed up and sat down on the top step of his porch, removing his hat and wiping his brow. "It's enough to send me to my grave, I tell you what, boys."

Sam nodded, like he completely understood the pain of trying to keep dandelions out of the yard. He wasn't sure why grown-ups made such a big deal about their grass. As long as it was mowed and flat enough to play sports on, he was happy.

CHAPTER TWO

S am looked back at the gray hat Mr. Haskins had been wearing. "Is that an old baseball cap?" It looked like the kind from the black-and-white highlight reels on ESPN.

"My what?" wheezed Mr. Haskins, patting his head until realizing that he was holding the hat in his other hand. He jerked back in surprise. "Oh—my hat. Well, let me tell ya boy, this hat is special."

"It is?" asked Sam, staring at the hat. It looked old, but not particularly special. It had a few small holes in the back, and the gray color was faded.

"This here is a genuine Confederate soldier's cap, yes it is." Mr. Haskins placed it gently back on his head, pulling the brim down toward his eyebrows.

"You mean, from the Civil War?" asked Sam.

"The War Between the States. Yep, that's the one," said Mr. Haskins.

"Wow, so it must be pretty old," said Derek.

"Of course it's old, boy!" cackled Mr. Haskins. "It was one hundred and fifty years ago, as a matter of fact. It's a milestone."

"Wow, that's older than you!" said Derek, smiling.

Mr. Haskins looked like he was about to shout something but then closed his lips tight together, obviously thinking better of it. "You should be so lucky," he muttered softly.

"But why do you have a Confederate Army hat?" asked Sam.

"Yeah, didn't they lose the Civil War?" said Derek.

Mr. Haskins' eyes opened wide. "Watch yourself, Yankee," he said in a fiery voice. "You're in the South now, don't forget. Richmond was the capital of the Confederacy."

"Oh, right," said Derek. "We're below Mr. Dixon's line."

"The Mason-Dixon line, boy!" Mr. Haskins raised his arm like he was going to smack Derek in the side of the head. "Get it right! Don't they teach you anything in that danged school of yours?"

Sam was pretty sure the Mason-Dixon line was the border between the North and South during the war, but he wasn't certain. When he lived back up north, he never really gave much thought to the Civil War, but here in Virginia, it was a much bigger deal. People seemed to really enjoy remembering history, maybe because there was so much of it around.

Sam looked back at the hat. "Do you act out Civil War battles or something?" He'd seen people dressed up like the founding fathers at St. John's Church in Richmond on a class trip last year, so maybe people did Civil War reenactments too.

"Nah," said Mr. Haskins. "Don't have the time for that kind of malarkey." Mr. Haskins paused, staring off at the trees like he was remembering something. "But there's no need to disrespect the South. A lot of blood was shed. A lot of young boys lost their lives. Sometimes, brother fought against brother on opposing sides of the battle. Some of them were not that much older than you two."

Sam hadn't really thought about having to go to war himself. He was pretty sure ten years old was too young to fight. Maybe Mr. Haskins meant Derek. Twelve wasn't old either, but his brother liked to act like he was already a teenager.

Mr. Haskins looked back over at them. "It's the anniversary, you know, of Lee's surrender at Appomattox —one hundred and fifty years."

"Apple what?" asked Derek.

"Appomattox!" barked Mr. Haskins. "Look it up! Open a book or turn on one of those electronic doodads you kids are always running around with. You might learn something!" He stood, turning toward his front porch. It looked like their conversation was over.

"Derek! Sam!" a voice called through the trees. "Come on, we're about ready to leave."

It was Mom, calling from their front yard.

"Let's go, Sam, we need to tell them goodbye," urged Derek, heading out of the yard. "See ya later, Mr. Haskins."

"Are they leaving you?" Mr. Haskins asked, nodding toward Sam's house.

"Mom and Dad are going to Paris for a week," Sam replied. "For their wedding anniversary." It was pretty extravagant, but their dad had won free airline tickets from a contest at work, and Mom had quickly arranged the trip. She said it was the trip of a lifetime.

"Paris?" Mr. Haskins put his hand on his chin and stared up at the clouds. "I was in Paris once. Beautiful city. The missus and I got lost in the Louvre for over thirteen hours. Nearly had to spend the night on the couch in Napoleon's apartment. Would have, too, if they hadn't found us when they did."

Sam didn't know what the heck the old man was talking about. He peered through the trees to make sure his mom and dad hadn't left yet.

"What are you boys going to do while they're gone? Try again to break my windows?"

"No, our cousin's coming to watch us. And we have lots of stuff lined up to do. Tomorrow we're riding bikes on Belle Isle." Sam turned, taking a few steps toward his house. "Okay, well…see ya."

"All right, boy. Happy trails on your bikes. Just keep a lookout for the ghosts."

Sam stopped in his tracks. He turned to the old man. "What?"

"On the island. Watch out for the ghosts."

Sam walked back over to where Mr. Haskins stood. "What ghosts?"

"You never heard the legend about the ghosts on Belle Isle?" Mr. Haskins shook his head in disbelief. "I tell you what, come over to my place later on and I'll tell you about the ghosts. Wouldn't kill you to sit still for a few minutes and listen for a change. Besides, if you're going to Belle Isle, you'll want to hear this."

Sam opened his eyes wide and gulped. Maybe he didn't want to know about the ghosts.

Mr. Haskins let out a cackle at the look on Sam's face. He slapped his wrinkly hand on Sam's shoulder, giving him a light shake. "Come on, boy, relax. Show some backbone. And bring that numbskull brother of yours, too."

Sam just nodded.

This was not going to be good.

CHAPTER THREE

"Honey, we're going to be late!" Dad's voice called as he lugged two black suitcases down the front steps. A few moments later, Mom dropped another bag in the foyer, but then disappeared. Sam pictured her consulting the giant notebook that housed all the lists she had made for every trip or vacation they'd ever taken.

A horn tooted behind them on the cul-de-sac as a taxi screeched to a stop at the end of their driveway. It wasn't yellow, like Sam would expect, but rather an ugly combination of green and white. A girl stepped out of the taxi and stood in front of them. She was older than them, and tall, with long, straight, black hair that flowed over her backpack.

"Honey, Meghan's here!" Dad called toward the house.

Meghan was their cousin, Aunt Darla and Uncle

Peter's daughter. Aunt Darla was their mom's sister, and they lived in upstate New York. Meghan was a sophomore at the University of Rochester, and now Mom and Dad's last-minute solution for a babysitter. It just so happened that Meghan's boyfriend, Paul, had graduated from college last spring and was now working in Richmond. Sam suspected he was the true reason Meghan had agreed to fly down and watch them, but he didn't say anything.

Paul was still at work, so Dad had arranged for a taxi to pick Meghan up from the airport. They were planning to take the same taxi for their trip so they didn't have to leave their car in the airport parking lot for a week. The whole plan was complicated. It was a good thing his mom had her list.

Sam didn't really remember Meghan. He'd been pretty young the last time they'd visited Aunt Darla's house before moving to Virginia. Mom had said Meghan was nineteen, which meant that she was still a teenager. He wasn't sure that was old enough to be responsible for them, but it was hard to tell. He thought he picked up a hint of doubt in Mom and Dad's voices at the decision, but they were pretty desperate and probably just happy to have someone they knew to watch them. He didn't want to think of who might have been their backup plan...maybe Mr. Haskins!

"Hi, Uncle Bill," said Meghan, as Sam's dad walked up.

"Hi there, Meghan," he answered, giving her a big hug. "Thanks for coming on such short notice! I'm not sure what we would have done without you."

"I told you that we could have taken care of ourselves, Dad," said Derek, walking up. He looked at Sam and chuckled. "Or at least, I could have. Sam might not have made it, but that wouldn't be a great loss."

"Hey, Derek," said Meghan, "You've certainly grown a lot. The last time I saw you, I think you were in kindergarten."

"Don't worry, he still acts the same," said Sam.

Meghan bent down farther than she needed to and looked into Sam's eyes. "Sam, You were just a little more than a baby the last time you came to my house in New York."

"Well, I'm ten now," said Sam, squirming uncomfortably as she tousled his hair.

Dad looked at his watch. "Well, I hate to throw you right into the fire, Meghan, but we've got a plane to catch. Alison's inside the house getting the last of the bags. Derek, why don't you grab Meghan's things and take her inside to Mom."

Derek picked up Meghan's suitcase, bowing to her like a butler. "Right this way, Madame. We've prepared a magnificent suite for you."

Meghan laughed, but Sam shook his head at Derek's antics. "Don't pay attention to him. He's always a little bit odd. Dad said they may have left him outside in the rain too long as a baby."

Derek led Meghan up to the front door. "Alison! I mean, Mom! Meghan's here!"

Sam looked over as his dad helped the driver load their bags into the taxi. He wished his parents weren't going away at all. Mom said it was important for them to have quality time for their marriage, whatever that meant. If they really wanted some quality time, they should just send Derek off to summer camp or something. That would make a very happy home as far as Sam was concerned.

"How long are you going to be gone again?" Sam asked, as the taxi driver slammed the green colored trunk shut with a bang.

"Just six days," said Dad, putting his arm on Sam's shoulder. "You're going to be okay, buddy. Mom's lined up a lot of fun things for you guys to do with Meghan and your friends while we're gone. We'll be home before you know it."

"I don't know why you have to go to Paris in the first place. Can't you just look at pictures on the Internet? It's almost the same thing."

"Sure," laughed Dad. "And you can just look at pictures of Yankee Stadium. I'm sure it would be exactly the same as sitting in the front row and catching a ball."

Sam grinned. His dad made a good point. As much as he loved reading about things in books and looking at pictures, he supposed there wasn't really anything like being someplace in person. "I guess," he conceded. "I just wish I could come with you."

"You'll have plenty of time to travel abroad when you're older," said Dad. "Besides, you guys always have so much fun exploring things around here. I have no doubt you'll stay busy. Just take it easy on Meghan, okay?"

Sam looked toward the house as Mom, Derek, and Meghan came out the door with a few small bags. He wasn't so sure about the whole Meghan thing. Maybe Mr. Haskins wouldn't be such a bad choice after all…

"Okay, Sam?" Dad repeated. "Promise me that you and your brother will behave and listen to Meghan."

"I will, Dad, I will," sighed Sam. "You should be telling that to Derek though. He's always the one causing trouble."

"Don't worry, I told him the same thing. Just do your part."

"Okay, I think this is everything," Mom announced, joining them at the end of the driveway. "Meghan, here is the extra set of keys for the house and the minivan. You have all our trip information on the paper by the refrigerator. And you can call Bill's brother, Drew, if you have any problems, too. They're only just outside of town."

"I've got it, Aunt Ali. Don't worry. You guys just enjoy yourself. We'll be fine." She shot a sweet smile over to the boys. Too sweet, Sam couldn't help but think.

"Mom, we'll be great. Don't worry," said Derek. "What's the worst that could happen?"

"Ha!" said Mom with a nervous laugh.

Derek flashed an innocent smile. "Now get going before you guys miss your flight."

"He's right, honey, we have to go," agreed Dad.

Mom bit her lip, then nodded. "Okay. Well, come here and give me hugs." It looked like she might be fighting back tears.

"Don't forget my snow globe of the Eiffel Tower!" called Derek as the driver started the engine.

Dad waved his hand out the window.

"Bon voyage!" called Meghan.

As the taxi pulled away, Sam, Derek, and Meghan stood alone at the top of the driveway.

"So…" said Sam, not knowing what to say.

"What are we going to do now?" asked Derek.

"Well," said Meghan. "Your mom said there's a pizza in the freezer for dinner tonight. And in the morning, you guys are going to go ride bikes on some island. You do know how to ride bikes on your own, right? I don't have to push you or anything, do I?" The sweet smile had disappeared from Meghan's face.

"Uh, yeah, we know how to ride bikes," said Derek.

Geez. How old did she think they were, five? "Aren't you going to come with us?" asked Sam.

"Actually, I'm supposed to meet my boyfriend, Paul, tomorrow morning, so I thought I could drop you off. Think you can handle that?"

A song erupted suddenly from Meghan's pocket. "Ooh, that's him now!" She pulled her cell phone out, excitedly tapping the screen. "Yes, I'm here. Can't wait to see you!" She turned up the driveway to the house, her ear to the phone. "You wouldn't believe all the things that they have lined up for me to do with these two…"

Sam looked over at Derek as Meghan's voice trailed off into the house. "I don't have a good feeling about her. Do you think she should leave us at Belle Isle alone? Mom and Dad would never do that."

"Are you kidding me?" Derek's face lit up. "This is going to be great! It's like a week of roaming free without Mom and Dad telling us what to do. You saw how Meghan acted as soon as they left. I think she's going to be more interested in talking to her boyfriend than watching us. It's perfect!"

CHAPTER FOUR

Once they had cleared away the dinner plates, the boys tumbled out of the house and ran up to Mr. Haskins' front porch.

Meghan didn't seem to mind them going over to Mr. Haskins' house after dinner. She was eagerly awaiting another call from Paul, even though they'd just talked before dinner. Sam knew girls were hard to understand, but he started to think that maybe college age girls were even harder.

Sam almost didn't tell Derek about Mr. Haskins' invitation after dinner. He wasn't sure he wanted to hear any ghost stories, and he knew that once Derek heard the word *ghost*, there would be no turning back. In the end, his own curiosity had won out since they were going to be on the island the next day.

"Come on, push the button!" said Derek, motioning Sam to the doorbell on Mr. Haskins' front porch.

"I did push it, nothing happened."

"Well, do it again."

"You do it again," said Sam, backing away from the door. "I don't want to keep ringing it and make him mad."

"Are you sure he invited us over?"

"Yes, I'm sure. He said—" Sam made his voice as deep and crusty as he could manage, "'—You boys come on over, and I'll tell you a tale.'"

Derek cracked up at Sam's imitation.

"Maybe he's sleeping," said Sam. "Or maybe he's going to the bathroom."

"For all this time?" said Derek.

"I don't know, he's old. Things take longer. Try knocking. Maybe the bell doesn't work."

Derek opened the screen and rapped on the wooden door with his knuckles sending flakes of paint fluttering to the ground. The door creaked open a few inches.

"Hello? Mr. Haskins?" said Derek, leaning into the dark space.

"I don't think he's here. Look, there's not even a car in the driveway," Sam pointed behind the house.

"Of course there's not a car, Sam. He doesn't drive anymore 'cause he's like 80 or 90 years old. Come on."

"But what if he sees us? He won't like us walking around his house."

"You said he invited us," said Derek, stepping into the room. "Why would he mind?"

Sam had only been inside Mr. Haskins' house a couple times since they'd moved in two summers ago. It looked even older on the inside than it did from the outside, like stepping into a black-and-white movie. It gave Sam the creeps. A musty smell hung in the air like a mixture of old socks and cough medicine.

"Anybody home?" Derek said again, the floorboards creaking under his footsteps.

"Mr. Haskins?" called Sam. "It's Sam and Derek Jackson...from next door...you told us to come over?"

"Maybe he's in the shower," said Derek. "I hope he's not naked."

"You think he'd shower with his clothes on?"

Derek laughed. "No! I hope he's not showering at all."

Sam tried not to picture Mr. Haskins in the shower. It was almost worse than thinking about ghosts.

"Get out of my house!" a voice hollered. Sam froze at the sound. "Come back here on the deck so I can talk to you!"

Sam let out a long breath, relieved to have found the old man. They walked to the back of the house, stepping out onto the wooden deck. Mr. Haskins was relaxing on a chair, sipping from a glass. He'd changed out of his robe but was still wearing the old civil war hat.

"I'd offer you some sweet tea, but I just finished it off," he explained, taking a long swallow from his glass. He motioned at two more wooden chairs beside him. A small table held a flickering mosquito repellent candle.

Sam felt a pinch in his skin and smacked his neck a second too late. He ducked into the chair quickly before he got attacked by any more bugs. The thought of anything sucking his blood made him squeamish.

For a minute, they all sat in the dusk in silence, staring into the candle flame. Sam hated small talk, and he never knew what was about to come out of Derek's mouth in situations like this.

"So, you're going to Belle Isle, are ya?" said Mr. Haskins, breaking the silence.

"Yep, we're going tomorrow to ride our bikes," said Derek.

"Have you been there?" asked Sam.

"Me?" the old man cackled. "Of course I've been there, boy. I've lived here my whole life." He slid back in his chair with narrowed eyes. "The more important question is, have *you*?"

"No, this will be our first time," answered Sam, hesitantly.

Mr. Haskins took a slow sip of his drink and leaned his head back against his chair, staring at the sky. "The first time I went to Belle Isle was back in 1947. I wasn't much older than you two. I wasn't riding bikes, mind you. Me and my best friend, Jimmy Howser, we were camping out on the north side of the island."

"I didn't know you could camp there," said Sam.

"Don't think you can, today," answered Mr. Haskins. "But back in '47, there weren't all the regulations and whatnot like there are today. Kids could roam around and do all kinds of exploring. Jimmy had an older sister with a place right near Belle Isle, so one night we snuck out with a knapsack and my BB gun to sleep under the stars."

"Did it rain?" asked Derek. "It almost always rains when we go camping."

"Quiet, boy," shushed Mr. Haskins, slapping Derek's knee. "Let me tell the story." He creaked further back into his chair. "Back during the Civil War, Belle Isle was a prisoner-of-war camp for Union soldiers."

Sam raised his eyebrows in surprise. "It was?" He'd never heard that before.

"Yes, sir. Terrible place, it was. Of course, I guess most prisons back then were pretty awful, but this one especially so. It's said that when some of the prisoners were released back to the Union army, the doctors found them in such bad shape, they were nearly dead." He paused, looking out into the woods. "They were like walking ghosts."

"Whoa," muttered Derek.

A slight breeze blew across the deck, just enough to ruffle Sam's hair, sending chills down his spine. He didn't like where this story was going, but he kept listening.

Mr. Haskins nodded, as if assuring them he spoke the truth. "Now, unlike most prisons, the camp on Belle Isle didn't have walls, just tents lined up in an open field."

"Wouldn't the prisoners just escape?" asked Sam. That didn't make any sense.

Mr. Haskins chuckled and folded his hands on his lap. "Well, tent walls made of canvas and rope don't sound like much until you consider that there were a hundred Confederate soldiers guarding the place. That and a row of cannons on the hill. They staked out a line on the ground called the dead zone. Any prisoner who crossed the line was shot on sight."

Yikes.

"Think that would be enough to make you stay?" asked Mr. Haskins.

"I think so," answered Sam.

"I bet I could've taken them," said Derek.

"Sure you could, tough guy," laughed Mr. Haskins. He took another long sip of his tea. "The island was a terrible place during the war. Afterward, they built a factory there where they made nails and things like that."

"I thought you said there were ghosts," said Derek, fidgeting in his seat.

"Be patient, boy. I'm getting to it." Mr. Haskins shifted his weight with a groan. "For years after the war, men working in the factory reported hearing noises, and at night, they'd see things out on the water."

Sam's heart was beating fast.

"What did they see?" asked Derek, leaning in.

The old man's voice grew quieter. "Lights. Floating out on the water. Some folks claimed they looked like the faces of Union soldiers—the ones who died in the prison camp but never received a proper burial."

"Why didn't they bury them?" asked Sam.

"Well, they may have dumped them in a shallow grave, but not with any kind of proper ceremony or stone markers. Nothing like Hollywood Cemetery, across the river. More than eighteen thousand Confederate soldiers are buried over there."

"Whoa," said Sam. "That's a lot of graves." He couldn't imagine that many people dying, let alone all buried in one place.

"So that's all people saw? Lights on the water?" Derek sounded unimpressed.

"Well, there's more to my story, but I can tell that you boys aren't interested," Mr. Haskins said, placing his drink on the table. "Maybe another time."

The boys bolted upright in their chairs. "No!" they shouted in unison. "We want to hear."

"You do, huh?" Mr. Haskins smiled. "Well, it's

common knowledge that the water on the James gets particularly stirred at night. Nobody knows why, but they grow fierce and wild. Then, each night, exactly at midnight, the ghosts of the Union and Confederate soldiers rise from their graves to battle on the rapids between the island and the cemetery. Flashes of light burst all around as their swords clash and the gunpowder fires from their rifles."

"Give me a break," said Derek. "If that's true, how come no one's ever taken a picture or a video of it?"

"Trust me, boy, many have tried, but the ghosts sense when folks are watching. Just like the Sasquatch. It's never been captured."

"Maybe because it isn't real, Mr. Haskins," said Sam, working hard to remind himself that the tale was fiction.

"Maybe it is, maybe it isn't," answered Mr. Haskins. "Just don't try to tell that to my friend Jimmy."

"Why not?" asked Derek. "Is he dead?"

"Yep."

"What?" said Sam, gripping the arms of his chair tightly.

"But because he was old, right?" said Derek.

Mr. Haskins' eyes narrowed. "Weren't natural causes that killed old Jimmy Howser, boys. In fact, that night camping on Belle Isle was the last time I ever saw him."

Sam let out a deep breath. This was getting to be too much. Mr. Haskins was just trying to scare him now. Sam looked over toward his house, wishing that Mom and Dad were home and not Meghan.

"What happened?" asked Derek.

"Well, Jimmy and I saw the lights on the water that night."

"You did?" said Sam.

"Yep. Now, I'll be honest with you boys, I couldn't be quite sure exactly what it was, but there was definitely something out there. I'll swear to it. We didn't sleep a wink that night, just kept thinking about those soldiers from the war lying underneath us in the ground. Just before dawn, we packed up our camp and hightailed it home."

"But what happened to Jimmy?" asked Sam.

"Well, Jimmy wouldn't give up on the idea that something was out there. He couldn't get what we saw on the water out of his mind. So a few nights later, he went back. He called me on the telephone, asking me to go with him, but I said no. I'd had enough of that island at night. But Jimmy went anyway. Alone. And he never came back."

The boys sat frozen in their chairs, hanging on Mr. Haskins' words. "Never?" asked Sam. "What happened to him?"

"Dunno. Next day, his pap called the police. I told them where Jimmy said he was going, and they searched the island top to bottom. Even dragged the river from boats, but they never found a body. It was like he vanished into the night. People started saying it must have been the ghosts that took him for nosing around in their business."

"Was it the ghosts?" asked Sam, eyes bugging out of his head.

"I don't know, boy. But I can tell you what I saw that first night, when I was hiding behind a rock on the shore of the James. There was an eerie light floating over the water where no light should have been. And I can tell you that I lost a good friend. That's what I do know."

Everyone sat silently, Mr. Haskins' words hanging in the air. Sam didn't know what to believe.

A loud bang smacked the table, sending Sam and Derek out of their chairs with a start.

"Gotcha, mosquito!" Mr. Haskins cackled. He looked up at the boys. "I didn't scare you two, did I?"

Sam stood up and moved to the steps. It was definitely time to go.

"Sure, I guess you boys ought to be getting home. That cousin of yours is probably wondering where you've run off to."

"Thanks for the story," Derek managed to say, looking as nervous as Sam felt.

"Don't mention it," grinned Mr. Haskins. "You two have fun on Belle Isle tomorrow, ya hear?"

CHAPTER FIVE

S am whipped along the dirt trail on his bike. He was moving fast—probably too fast from the way the trees were flying by him. He was trying to keep up with Derek, not wanting to be riding through the narrow paths by himself.

There were two types of trails on Belle Isle. A wide, oval-shaped, walking trail ran around the perimeter, while more advanced trails cut through the middle of the island. The narrower paths were littered with steep climbs and drops, just wide enough for a single hiker or rider. Sam preferred the less treacherous, wider trails on the outside loop, but Derek kept leading him farther into the interior maze.

Belle Isle was right on the edge of the city, although looking around at the woods and the rapids, Sam felt he could be a hundred miles away from Richmond. The James River flowed around both sides of the island, but the two sides were starkly different. The north side pressed right up against the rapids, with fast-moving water coming right up to the shore in some spots. When the river was high, one false move and a biker could be washed away in the current. The south side was a shallow trickle of water spread among an expanse of flat rocks.

Being on the island reminded him of the time his dad took him into New York City for a baseball game. Before the game, they had hiked around Central Park. Sam couldn't believe there were such secluded places in the biggest city in the country. He remembered thinking he wouldn't want to be in Central Park alone at night. After Mr. Haskins' story about camping on the island, he now had the same feeling about Belle Isle.

His back tire slid around another blind corner, but then he finally saw Derek's bike up ahead, leaning against a washing-machine-sized boulder on the side of the trail. Sam braked, steadying himself with one foot on the ground. Sweat dripped down his face as he unbuckled his bike helmet. It was still morning, but July in Virginia was always hot.

He leaned his bike next to Derek's on the rock, glancing around the thick woods for his brother. Where had he gone now? A narrow path led from the bike trail, and Sam followed it to the ruins of an old brick building.

Giant vines and ivy scaled the crusty bricks of a lone wall, probably fifty feet long, the only remnant of a building now long gone. Pieces were missing from the wall, a victim of time and too many mischievous visitors. A green heart was spray painted on the bricks next to a wide archway that had once served as a door.

Sam wandered along the wall, gazing at the decades of wear written on the bricks. He thought about the island being a prisoner-of-war camp. An informational sign by the bridge had proved that part of Mr. Haskins' story to be true. He wondered how many prisoners had tried to escape. How many had been shot? Maybe the whole island really *was* a graveyard. It gave him the creeps just thinking about it.

"Hey, what are you doing there?!" a voice yelled out.

Sam jumped in surprise, but quickly realized it was just Derek. His brother sauntered out from behind one of the brick archways, a smile stretched wide across his face.

"What's the matter, Sam? You look like you saw a ghost!"

"How'd you like to *be* a ghost? Why do you have to scare me like that? I've been looking all over for you."

"I'm sorry, man. Geez. Nature called, you know what I mean? If you gotta go, you gotta go."

Sam stepped away from the wall. "You could have waited for me."

"Sure, next time I'll make an announcement across the whole island that I've got to pee."

"Perfect, thanks," said Sam, turning toward the bikes. "Let's get out of here."

"Hang on," said Derek. "You won't believe what I found down this hidden trail back here." Derek jumped back behind the wall out of sight.

"What is it?" Sam asked.

"Just come on. You have to see."

Sam reluctantly followed. He'd rather not take Derek's word for anything, but he wasn't going to stand next to that creepy wall in the woods by himself. The best way to avoid surprises was usually to keep Derek where he could see him.

Sam followed Derek along another narrow dirt path in the direction of the river. He strained his eyes to see a clearing through the tree branches. An old building loomed ahead, its walls partially covered with vines and graffiti.

"What is this place, Derek?"

"I think it's the old hydro plant. Remember Alex telling us about it on the bus last spring?"

"Oh, yeah," said Sam. The hydroelectric plant had used fast-moving water to make electricity. From the looks of things, it hadn't been used for a long time.

There were windows and doors in the walls, but iron bars blocked them like an old prison cell. Dark shadows from the trees made the whole place look spooky.

"Are we supposed to be back here?" asked Sam.

"It looks like somebody else was. Check it out." Derek pointed through the bars of the doorway. Cigarette butts and empty beer bottles were scattered in a corner. "It's like a hideout."

"Not anyplace I'd like to hide," said Sam, peering through the bars. He could see into an open room with a high ceiling stretched thirty feet above him. He pulled his head back to see Derek climbing through an opening in the metal bars at the top of the doorway.

"What are you doing? Get down!" called Sam.

Derek ignored him sliding his leg over the top bar and dropping down to the dirt floor on the other side. He grabbed onto the metal bars shaking them with a desperate look on his face. "I'm innocent! Innocent, I tell ya!"

"Quit it," said Sam, rolling his eyes. "If somebody comes along, you're gonna get us both in trouble." Despite his anxiety, Sam had to admit the building was pretty cool. The crumbling walls and ceiling reminded him of a scene from the Spider-Man movie they'd seen last summer. He shivered at the thought of an evil creature emerging from the shadows.

Derek was already studying three rectangular concrete shapes, framed in rusty iron in the middle of the dirt floor. "I bet these held the power generators." He moved to the middle wall where three circular, metal sections, about six feet across, lined up evenly with each of the shapes in the floor. From where Sam was standing, they looked like huge air lock doors in a submarine. But instead of a handle at the center, each section had a circular opening.

Derek traced one of the openings with his hand. "I bet something went from the generators on the floor over there and into these circles to control the water." He bent down and felt the dirt on the floor. "It's almost like sand. There must have been a lot of water moving through here."

Sam imagined water suddenly filling the room—thousands of gallons rushing through the openings in the wall. It would wash Derek right into the river, or maybe chop him up in the electric turbines.

Derek climbed through one of the center holes, landing in the adjoining room. "Get in here. You have to see this. There's something written over here."

"What is it?" said Sam. He didn't want to get in there. He wanted to leave. But he knew Derek wouldn't leave until he came in and looked, so he placed a foot onto the metal bars and started scaling the side of the building like he'd seen Derek do. As he draped his leg over the opening at the top, he glanced down and felt dizzy. He was only about twelve feet up, but it seemed higher. He closed his eyes to block out the height as he swung a leg over the top bar and inched one foothold at a time down the other side.

He breathed a sigh of relief when his shoes crunched on the room's loose gravel. When he leaned his head through the opening Derek had climbed through, he saw Derek staring at the far wall.

"What do you see?" asked Sam.

Derek didn't answer, so Sam climbed through the opening, his legs scraping against the rusty metal edges. He wondered what kind of terrible disease he could catch from this place. "What is so awesome that you can't—" He stopped mid-sentence as saw the wall. "Oh, man… what is that?"

He stepped next to Derek so he could get a better view of the entire wall. A huge painting, like a mural, covered the wall from the floor to the ceiling. A twenty-foot-high picture of a shadowy rounded head with deep scary eyes stared back at him.

"It looks like a ghost, doesn't it?" said Derek.

"We need to get out of here, now," said Sam, backing away. "Beer bottles, cigarettes, walls with ghosts, this can't be good. Kids didn't make this. This is a grownup place, and I don't want to be here when they get back." He tried to force the word *ghost* out of his mind.

Derek waved his hand. "Relax, this could be from a long time ago. It's probably a hundred years old. I'll bet no one even knows it's here. You can't see it from the trails."

"Exactly," answered Sam. "A secluded spot in the woods. It's the kinds of place where bad things happen. Don't you watch TV? Who knows what kind of crazy psycho might live out here? There's a reason why there are bars on the windows and doors. We're not supposed to be in here."

"Sam, there you go with your—" Derek suddenly stopped talking, holding his hand up at the same time. "Did you hear that?" he whispered.

"Very funny. You don't have to make fun of me. Let's just get out of here."

"Shh. I'm not kidding." Derek's face looked dead serious. "Listen. Voices."

Sam stopped arguing and listened. He did hear voices faintly echoing below the room. This was just what he was afraid of. "We have to get out of here!"

"Shh!" Derek hissed. "Be quiet and follow me." He rushed back to the metal opening and climbed through.

The voices were getting louder. Sam could hear feet clomping up metal stairs. There must be an entrance on the river side that they hadn't seen. He followed Derek through the opening, raising his legs carefully over the rusty corners. As he slid into the first room, Derek was already halfway up the bars on the doorway. Sam didn't have time to think about being scared of the height now. He just leaped onto the metal and climbed.

As Sam swung his leg over the top, a loud metallic groan came from inside the other room. Men's voices were loud now, and he realized there must be a staircase with a metal trap door into the room. He turned to scurry down the outside of the bars when something stopped his leg. Fear zipped through his body. He looked to see who had grabbed him, but it was only his shoelace, caught on a sharp piece of the metal.

"Come on, Sam!" Derek was already standing on the trail, motioning to him.

Sam reached back and pulled at the lace, but it wouldn't come loose. The voices were in the next room now, so he pulled the shoe off his foot, freeing the lace, and threw it down to the ground. He slipped down the remaining bars until he reached the earth and raced over to Derek at the edge of the woods, relieved that he hadn't fallen and broken his neck.

For once, Derek seemed content to leave without finding out what was going on, and they ran quickly but quietly up the trail they'd come in on.

"Let's go," said Derek as they reached their bikes. Sam didn't argue as he kicked his pedals in motion. Soon they were back on the trail, tearing through the woods faster than ever.

At a split in the trail, Sam hesitated on which way to go. Derek had pulled ahead again and was out of sight. To the left seemed flatter, but it was the long way around the island. Sam didn't want to go the long way. He wanted to catch up with Derek and get home. He was all done exploring Belle Isle. To the right seemed quicker, but it was a steep trail down. He imagined what Derek would say to him if he were there. He'd probably call Sam a chicken or something.

Sam decided to be brave and chose the steep path, firmly squeezing the right hand brake to the rear tire, with his left hand ready to spring to action on the front tire brake if he needed to stop quickly. As he descended the steepest part, he tried to keep his balance and let the bike do the work. He refused to look to the right, where the edge of the path had eroded over the side of the hill.

Halfway down the slope, he saw Derek waiting at the bottom. Sam breathed a sigh of relief and continued down the steep grade with more confidence.

"Sam, look out!" Derek suddenly shouted, pointing up the hill to Sam's left.

Sam turned to look, but before he had time to squeeze his hand brake, three blurs of motion cut in front of him with a yell. Sam was so surprised that he jerked his handlebars to the right to avoid a crash.

"Watch out, kid!" Three teenagers on bikes buzzed on down the trail, their tires kicking dirt up in Sam's face.

Sam's front wheel slipped over the edge of the incline,

sending him and his bike hurtling down the side of the hill like a one-man runaway train. "Whoa!" he cried as he fishtailed through the undergrowth, gaining speed toward a big rock. In a panic he squeezed both brakes at once, locking up his front wheel, and sending him flying over the handlebars.

CHAPTER SIX

S am felt like he was in slow motion as he sailed through the air. Derek's mouth was open wide in a yell, his hands waving like a second base cut-off man. The three teenagers had skidded to a stop next to Derek and were doubled over laughing. Time spun back into regular speed as Sam landed hard on the far edge of the lower trail. He rolled twice before coming to a stop in the weeds.

"Sam!" yelled Derek, rushing over. "Are you all right?"

Sam spit a wad of dirt and gravel out of his mouth. "I think so," he groaned, sitting up slowly and unbuckling his helmet strap. His knee throbbed and blood was dripping from his arm, but at least he was alive. His bike was perched at an angle against the big rock on the hill.

"Nice job, daredevil!" one of the teenagers laughed.

The boy turned to Derek. "Hey, Jackson, you know this little squirt? Hope you didn't teach him how to ride a bike."

"Shut up, Cameron," said Derek. "Just leave him alone, will you? Why don't you guys watch where you're riding?" Derek pulled Sam off the ground gently. "Can you walk?"

"I think so." Sam pushed his hand against the ground and stood. His right leg and arm were covered in an ugly mix of blood and gravel.

"Watch where you're going, kid," one of the boys cackled. "Next time you cross our path, you might not be so lucky."

Sam shot the three teenagers as mean a glare as he could muster.

"What? Don't believe us? Just ask your brother what it's like in big-boy school. Enjoy your summer, Jackson. Rest up. September will be here before you know it."

Derek helped Sam brush off, ignoring the other boys as they rode away.

"See ya soon, Jackson!" one of them screamed, as they rode away down the path.

Derek retrieved Sam's bike from the hill, setting it on the trail. Sam spun the front wheel, revealing a slight wobble, but it seemed rideable. "Whoa, look at your helmet! It's cracked!" said Derek, pointing at Sam's head.

Sam held it up for inspection. Sure enough, right on

top was a big crack in the plastic. "Better the helmet than me, I guess."

"Can you ride?" asked Derek.

"I think I'm okay, if we go slow." Sam strapped on his cracked helmet and climbed onto his bike. He looked up at the trail to where the boys had ridden off and then back at his brother. "Who were those guys, Derek?"

Derek's face hardened and he started off along the dirt trail. "Nobody, just forget it," he called over his shoulder.

Sam struggled to keep up. "Slow down. I don't want my wheel to fall off." Derek slowed the pace and Sam peddled up next to him. "No really, do they go to your school?" It was weird. Derek was always the big kid wherever he went. Sam had never seen him made fun of like that.

Derek stopped his bike, putting a foot down in the dirt. "It's just Cameron Talley and his buddies. They're idiots." He looked off into the woods, shaking his head. "Believe it or not, some things in middle school aren't as great as you'd think they would be."

"What did they do, give you the royal flush and then stuff you in your locker?" Sam remembered reading that in a book one time, how bullies picked you up and put your head in the toilet bowl as it flushed. Pretty mean—and disgusting.

Derek shot him an annoyed glance. "No, they don't

do that. They just give some of the younger kids a hard time—especially me. I don't know why. They think they're so cool. I think they're just trying to show off." He let out a deep breath then looked down at Sam and started laughing. "Dude, you really look terrible! You're going to have to wash your leg in the river before anyone sees you."

"Well how do you think I'd look after a crash like that?" said Sam.

Derek laughed. "You're lucky you weren't hurt worse. You had massive air!" He pushed down on his pedal. "Come on, let's get back to the bridge so we'll be there when Meghan comes to pick us up. If you can make it, that is."

"I'll make it," said Sam. "Just go slow, okay?"

They rode the trail all the way to the long suspension bridge at the front of the island. It was unlike any walking bridge Sam had ever seen, hanging from enormous steel cables underneath a tall highway overpass. The bridge was made of six-foot-wide concrete sections that rose and fell in long arching patterns.

While he knew it was probably safe, since so many people walked and rode bikes across the span, the bridge's odd shape made him nervous. He tried to ride in the middle, but he often had to move toward the edge to avoid other bikes and people walking their dogs. The slight wobble in his tire wasn't helping his confidence level, and too often he found himself staring into the waters below.

When they finally reached the end of the bridge, Meghan was parked on the side of the road, talking on the phone as usual. Mom and Dad had arranged for her to drop Sam off at the bookstore downtown while Derek went to soccer practice. Both of them loved to stop at a bookstore for new reading material. Derek loved mysteries, while Sam preferred adventures.

This bookstore was special, since it was owned by Mrs. Murphy, Sam's friend Caitlin's mom. Caitlin helped her mom at the store every Tuesday over the summer. Sam had thought it sounded pretty boring to just sit around a bookstore all day with nothing to do, but after a visit, he decided it looked fun. The store was filled with rows and rows of cool kids' books and comfy couches to read them on. Caitlin got to read whatever she wanted, but she also helped to restock shelves and unpack shipments of books, which meant she got to see all the new books first.

Mrs. Murphy had invited Sam to spend a few hours that day helping Caitlin out at the store. Afterward, they would go back to their house for dinner and watch a movie. Sam normally avoided girls, but Caitlin had become a good friend ever since she'd helped him and Derek out with the mystery over at Church Hill and in Williamsburg. Derek had teased that Sam was going on a date, but Sam ignored him. Caitlin used to act like a real know-it-all, but now even Derek admitted she was pretty cool.

Meghan dropped Sam off at the curb in front of the store. Derek waved out the window like a goofy maniac as they pulled away, acting as if they'd never see each other again. Sam grinned and walked into the shop.

A bell rang as Sam entered the bookstore. Mrs. Murphy waved from behind the counter as she scanned another customer's purchases. "Hi, Sam! Caitlin's upstairs in the office. You can go on up, if you like."

"Thanks, Mrs. Murphy." He hurried down one of the dozen or so rows of books before she could question him about his injuries. Meghan, not surprisingly, hadn't noticed.

Sam wondered how Mrs. Murphy could ever hope to sell all these books. There never seemed to be many customers when he visited and there were always boxes of new books arriving. He supposed it gave folks a good selection, but it would probably take ten lifetimes to read every book in the place.

"Sam Jackson, please report to the mystery aisle," a voice echoed through the store. "Sam Jackson, please report to mysteries."

Sam looked up and saw Caitlin waving at the top of the stairs from behind the bookshelves. Her sandy blonde hair was blowing in her face under the air conditioning vent. She pushed her hair away from her eyes, grinning behind a microphone that was connected to the store speakers. She ducked back through the office door as Sam walked over to the mystery aisle.

All the books in the store were set up by category —*genre*, as Caitlin called it when she was trying to act smart. Sam ran his fingers over the brightly colored spines, remembering that Mom had left only enough money for him to buy one book.

"Ooh, that's a scary one," a voice came from behind the shelf. Sam leaned over to see a blue eye staring back from a space between two books. Caitlin giggled and came around the corner. "Hey, how are ya?"

"I'm okay," said Sam. "How's it going working in the bookstore?"

"I like it. There are so many interesting things to look at and read. Plus, a lot of other kids come in for books, so I get to talk to them, too. Billy actually came in this morning. I hadn't seen him since school ended."

"Wow. I didn't think he knew how to read," joked Sam. Billy Maxwell was another kid in their grade. He tended to be obnoxious. He and Caitlin used to really hate each other, but they were starting to get along better. Maybe Billy was maturing, or Caitlin was mellowing out. Probably some of both.

"Yeah, I think he just looked at the picture books,"

laughed Caitlin, walking closer. "Oh, Sam, what happened to your arm? It's bleeding!"

"Well … I had a little mishap at Belle Isle on my bike," replied Sam, sheepishly. He wasn't sure whether crashing on his bike made him sound rugged or weak, but there was no hiding the blood on his arm. He told Caitlin about the teenagers that had cut him off, and how they had been bullying Derek at school.

"What jerks," huffed Caitlin. "I don't know why guys have to act like that, always trying to be so tough."

"I know, I didn't think that could ever happen to Derek. He always acts so cool around everyone else. I never figured him to be the one being picked on. I guess things are different in middle school." Sam thought about how he was only a year away from middle school himself. "I'm not looking forward to it."

"We'll be okay. You have lots of friends who will be going with you. I'm sure things will get better for Derek, too." She grimaced at the blood on Sam's arm. "Why don't you go wash your arm off in the bathroom? It's under the stairs over there next to the biography section. There might even be Band-Aids in the cabinet. Then I want to show you a new book about coins that my mom just got in. I think it has some pictures of an Indian Head cent like the one you found."

Sam walked over to the bathroom, happy to think about coins rather than bike crashes and middle school bullies. He and Derek had found a stolen collection of rare coins in the woods behind their house when they first moved to Virginia. Ever since, he'd been growing his personal coin collection, although he had nothing close to the value of the rare 1877 Indian Head cent they'd found in the woods. That one could be worth thousands. It was too bad they'd had to give it back to the museum.

After Sam got cleaned up, he spent the rest of the afternoon with Caitlin looking at books and talking about friends from school. It was weird, when they were in school, they couldn't wait for summer vacation, but during the summer, they spent lots of time talking about school. Sam decided it was a lot more fun to talk about school than to actually be there.

Before long, Mrs. Murphy said it was time to close up the store and head home for dinner. Sam brought one of the books he'd been looking at over to the register.

"Will there be anything else, sir?" Caitlin said, moving behind the counter to the register.

"Seriously?" asked Sam.

"Seriously. Hmm … I don't think we have anything by that title, sir. However, you might check in the humor section to be sure."

Sam made a goofy face at her lame joke as he handed her his book. Apparently, she knew how to operate the register, so he played along.

"Ah, submarines, very exciting. I highly recommend

this book." Caitlin punched a few numbers into the register. "That will be eight hundred and thirty-nine dollars, sir."

Sam's jaw dropped at the price. "Eight hundred dollars! What are the pages made of, gold?"

"Oops!" Caitlin leaned in, studying the screen closely as she tried to keep a straight face. "Aha! My mistake, sir. That should be eight dollars and thirty-nine cents." She looked back up at him confidently.

"That's more like it," said Sam.

"Will that be cash or charge?" She couldn't hold it in any longer and broke out giggling.

Sam patted his pockets. "Why, I seem to have left my credit cards at home, but I did bring my penny collection, will that be okay?"

Caitlin made a shocked face as he pretended to lift a huge bag of coins onto the counter. He laughed, finally handing her a ten-dollar bill. "I may have to report you to management, lady."

Caitlin dropped a dollar and some coins in his hand. "Thanks for shopping with us today, sir. Please come again!"

Sam and Caitlin walked out of the bookstore and onto the tree-lined sidewalk while Mrs. Murphy locked up in the back alley. Sam began flipping through his new book. He hardly ever made it all the way home without peeking. Uncovering a new adventure was too tempting to wait. Despite stumbling upon several real-life mysteries with Derek, it was still fun to read about them. Besides, the books were like training manuals for their true adventures down the road.

He stared at the gray submarine motoring past a colorful coral reef on the book cover. He imagined joining the crew inside the sub, just like in *20,000 Leagues Under the Sea*, which Dad had read them at bedtime a few years ago. He studied the rich detail of the picture, noticing for the first time a pair of eyes lurking in a dark cave in the corner.

"Sweet! Caitlin, look at this!" He held the book out to her just as a loud noise sounded on the street. Sam wasn't watching where he was going, and his foot accidentally slipped off the sidewalk into the street.

"Look out!" screamed Caitlin.

CHAPTER SEVEN

A high-pitched horn blared as a loud motor roared up. Sam jumped back as a motorcycle buzzed by him, knocking the book out of his hand.

"Get out of the road, kid!" growled the motorcycle rider, turning and shaking his fist in Sam's direction.

Caitlin grabbed Sam's arm, yanking him back to the sidewalk. "Are you okay?" She leaned over to pick up his book.

Sam's heart was beating fast. He had almost been roadkill. He stared at the biker rumbling on down the street. He looked tough. He was wearing black leather pants and boots, a leather vest, but no shirt underneath. Colorful tattoos were scattered over muscular arms that looked like they belonged to a football linebacker. Long hair waved from underneath a black helmet decorated with a red flag with a star-filled 'X' on it. He looked like the kind of guy you didn't want to meet in a dark alley— or anywhere, actually.

"Wow, look over there!" exclaimed Caitlin, pointing up the street.

As Sam had been staring at the man on the motorcycle, a sound, like a giant swarm of bees, had been growing louder and louder behind him. He turned to see an enormous parade of bikers approaching. There were dozens of them, several with red flags just like the one on the first rider's helmet waving behind their bikes.

"What is that flag they're carrying?" asked Sam. "I know I've seen it, but I can't remember where."

"Sam! Even you should know that. It's the Confederate flag. Don't you remember learning about that in class?" She looked at him with one of her know-it-all glances that used to drive him crazy.

"Oh, yeah," said Sam. There had only been a few weeks of summer vacation so far, but his memory of school was already fading from his brain. He remembered now that it was the flag of the Confederate States in the Civil War. He looked back at the bikers. "What are they doing, having a parade?"

"Looks like it. They're all stopping down there around that statue." She pointed to a traffic circle farther down the street. In the middle was a tall statue. The procession was looping around the statue, flags waving enthusiastically.

"What's all the commotion?" asked Mrs. Murphy, walking up the sidewalk. She turned to where Sam and Caitlin were looking and groaned. "Oh. There they go again. Causing a ruckus through town."

"Is that a biker gang?" asked Sam.

Mrs. Murphy huffed. "You could say that."

"What are they doing?" asked Caitlin.

"Celebrating their right to congregate," answered Mrs. Murphy.

"Congregate?" said Sam. "What does that mean?"

"It means they're meeting together, probably having a rally," said Mrs. Murphy. "They're loosely affiliated with an old historic group called the Ghosts of the Confederacy. I say loosely, because rumor has it they're more interested in drinking, fighting, and causing trouble than ever having a meeting."

Sam gulped at the name *Ghosts*. That word had been coming up a lot lately.

"Confederate Ghosts?" said Caitlin. "Is that why they have the Confederate flag on their helmets?"

"That's right, honey. This year is the hundred and fiftieth anniversary of the end of the Civil War. Although it seems like somebody's always interested in still fighting it."

"They want to fight the Civil War again?" asked Sam. He couldn't imagine why anyone would want to do that.

"No, not literally, Sam," answered Mrs. Murphy. "I

think many of them just use it as an excuse to have a party. A lot of folks like to hold onto the past, which can be a good thing or a bad thing. The smart ones try to learn from it, but others do it just to stir up trouble."

"Daddy says those people are just ignorant. Right, Mom?"

Mrs. Murphy laughed. "That's a good word for it sometimes, honey."

"What's that statue they're all circling?" asked Sam.

"The General? Oh, come on now, Sam. I know your family is from the North, but surely y'all know about General Robert E. Lee? He was the commander of the Southern troops."

"Oh, sure, I've heard of him," fudged Sam, nodding his head. The name did sound familiar, although he hoped Caitlin wouldn't ask him right then to explain. He wasn't always good at recalling details on command.

Mrs. Murphy laughed, patting him on the shoulder good-naturedly. "We need to get you educated on Southern history, Sam. Richmond was the capital of the Confederacy, you know. The South had its own currency, its own president, even its own White House for a time."

Sam remembered hearing Mr. Haskins say Richmond was the capital of the Confederacy, but hadn't known about the other stuff. "Wait a minute, I thought the White House was in Washington, D.C. And wasn't Abraham Lincoln the president during the Civil War?"

"All true," said Mrs. Murphy, "but eleven southern states seceded, declaring they were no longer part of our country. They formed the Confederate States of America and named Jefferson Davis as their president."

"Wow," said Sam. That sounded pretty serious. "No wonder it started a war."

"Can we go home now?" said Caitlin. "I'm getting hungry." She turned and smirked at Sam. "We can't teach him everything about the South in one afternoon."

"Hey, you didn't know all of those things either." Sam said. His brain was starting to spin, but if Caitlin thought it was time to stop talking about history, it must really be time to stop.

"Okay, maybe there was *one* thing I didn't know," replied Caitlin.

"Only one, honey?" said Mrs. Murphy. "How humble of you."

Caitlin's cheeks turned red. "Mom!"

CHAPTER EIGHT

L ater that night, Sam was back home and getting ready for bed. He stood next to Derek at the bathroom sink, both of them brushing their teeth. They'd shared one room with bunk beds when they first moved in. It had been fun talking to each other in bed at night, listening to the wind blow through the tall trees outside, but after a while, they had started getting on each other's nerves. Sometimes Sam just wanted to be alone. Mom and Dad finally agreed to split them up, moving Sam to the extra guest room.

The bathroom had doors on both ends, providing direct access to their two bedrooms. Mom called it a Jack-and-Jill layout, which seemed like a stupid name. Of course, Derek immediately began saying his room was the 'Jack' and Sam's was the 'Jill.' Now Sam just wished he had a private bathroom.

Derek finished brushing and stood shirtless in his pajama pants, admiring himself in the mirror. "So how was your date?"

Sam nearly choked on his toothpaste, glaring up at his brother in the mirror. "Shut up," he gurgled. "It wasn't a date."

"Did you have dinner?"

"Yeah."

"Did you watch a movie?"

"Sure, but—"

"Sounds like a date to me," Derek said, laughing. "What movie did you watch?"

Sam spit into the sink, wiping his mouth on a towel. He was about to argue further, but decided to let it go. "E.T. It was really good."

"Did you cuddle?"

"That's it!" Sam grabbed Derek's arm and moved in for a bear hug. Derek reacted quickly, wriggling loose, pushing Sam into the sink counter. His toothbrush slipped off the edge, sinking straight into the open toilet.

"Derek!" Sam screamed.

"What? I didn't do it. You attacked me. It's not my fault you gave your own toothbrush a royal flush."

Sam grimaced and let out a long sigh.

"Admit it, I'm just too strong for you!" said Derek, making a muscle with his arm. "Ooh, look at that."

Sam fished his toothbrush out of the toilet bowl,

rinsing it thoroughly under the sink faucet. "Look at what?" he mocked.

"My muscle. You can't handle my guns." Derek raised his arms up to his head and kissed his "guns" like a professional wrestler.

All Sam saw was Derek's regular, skinny arms. He looked away in disgust, still annoyed by his brother calling his time with Caitlin a date, not to mention his toothbrush flying into the toilet.

Derek had to be the cockiest twelve-year-old around. Mom and Dad always said they dreaded the day both of them would be teenagers given all the mischief they seemed to get into already. Now that Derek was in middle school, he seemed more convinced than ever that he was super tough and super cool. More like super annoying. All of which made it even more surprising that Cameron and the other guys had been hassling him earlier.

Sam walked into his room, more grateful than ever for his own space. Lying on his bed, he thought about what Mr. Haskins had said about brother fighting against brother in the Civil War. He glanced over at Derek's room, thinking he might like to battle it out with his brother occasionally. Not for real, though. Not with actual weapons and to the death.

Sam had never thought much about being a soldier, but it seemed scary. He knew it was important to have people who were soldiers to keep everyone safe, but he was happy to let somebody else do that. Did that make him a chicken? He wasn't sure. He didn't know what he wanted to be when he grew up, other than a professional baseball player, but he was pretty sure *soldier* would be far down the list.

He got up and sat down next to his bookcase, searching the titles until he found a thick hardcover called *The History of the World for Kids*, which his uncle Drew had bought him. He was always buying them books. Sam wasn't sure why. He guessed it had something to do with Uncle Drew being a teacher. Some of the books were a little strange, but most were interesting.

Sam especially liked this one. It had page after page of pictures and descriptions of important things and events in history, like the Egyptian pyramids, the Apollo moon landing, and all the major wars. He flipped through the pages until he reached the section on the Civil War. There were several grainy, black-and-white photos. One was of two tall, thin men looking serious in front of a cannon. Another showed a wooden fence and a wide field, with dead bodies scattered in the grass. Across the page, he spied something he recognized.

"It's General Lee," he said aloud. It was a picture of the Robert E. Lee statue from Monument Avenue. He was sure of it.

"The General Lee?" Derek asked, walking into the

room through the bathroom door. "You found a picture of the car? I love it how it makes all those cool jumps! I'm going to get a sweet sports car like that when I get my license in a few years."

Sam looked up from his book. Derek was always barging into places unexpectedly. The car that he was talking about was from an old TV show called *The Dukes of Hazzard* that they'd seen at their grandpa's house before they'd moved. An orange car the characters had named the General Lee was always getting chased by the cops and doing all sorts of crazy maneuvers. Grandpa loved it for some reason, but it always seemed a little silly to Sam. Although, it was cool how the car doors never opened and the guys always slid in through the windows. He didn't think Mom and Dad would like it much if he tried to do that in their minivan. He probably couldn't even jump that high.

Sam frowned. "Don't you ever knock?"

"The door was open," said Derek, innocently. "What are you looking at?" He leaned down and snatched the book from Sam's hands. "Oh, I love this book."

"Hey, I'm looking at it!" Sam grabbed it back and socked his brother on the shoulder. "Get out of here!"

"Okay, okay," Derek backed away, but he sat down on Sam's bed instead of leaving. "I'm sorry, dude. Relax. Seriously, what are you looking at?"

Sam took a breath and tried to focus back on his

book. "I'm looking at this chapter about the Civil War. Right here is a picture of the General Robert E. Lee statue I saw today outside Mrs. Murphy's bookstore. It was while you were at soccer practice. On the way home she drove us all the way down Monument Avenue. It was filled with statues on nearly every block. It was crazy." He described to Derek the biker gang and the rally around the Lee monument. "It got me thinking about what Mr. Haskins said about brothers fighting against brothers in the Civil War."

Derek stood up in the middle of the room and began dancing back and forth like a boxer, raising his fists. "It could have been us, Sam, fighting to the death!" He threw a pretend punch to Sam's chin.

"It wasn't a fist fight," said Sam, standing up. "But if it was, I'd be in the Northern Army." He dodged a left hook from his brother. "You'd lose."

"Ha!" Derek threw a phantom punch at Sam's chest. "Well, then I'd get the General Lee and do awesome car jumps." He hit Sam's stomach with a sneaky jab and scampered back to his room before Sam could retaliate. "Retreat!"

Sam sat down on his rug to read more from his book, keeping watch out of the corner of his eye in case Derek came back. It said that Lee's army defended Richmond against the Union army, led by General Ulysses S. Grant, for ten months. In early 1865, Lee's troops evacuated, sending the city into chaos. Supplies of whiskey were set on fire, artillery exploded at the Tredegar Ironworks factory where they made the ammunition, and the panicked people rioted and looted. Before long, more than fifty blocks of the city were on fire. The only thing that saved the rest of Richmond from destruction was the Union Army marching in the next morning and putting out the fires.

Sam stopped reading. He tried to picture the city in flames, just like Mr. Haskins had imagined his dandelion-filled yard.

"Hey, I just have one more question," Derek interrupted, sticking his head through the doorway again.

Sam sighed and closed the book, looking up at his brother. "What is it?"

"Did you kiss her?"

"Will you get out of here?!" Sam grabbed a pillow off the floor next to him, heaving it at the doorway.

Derek pulled back just in time, and the pillow crashed up against a Yankees poster on the wall. "Missed me!" he laughed, slamming the door shut before Sam could reload.

He didn't need a separate room, he needed a separate house!

CHAPTER NINE

The next morning, the boys were outside playing catch in the yard when a white SUV pulled up to their house.

"Who is that?" asked Derek, lowering his glove.

Before Sam could answer, the back door opened and Caitlin jumped out. "Hey, guys!"

Derek tapped Sam on the shoulder and gave him an obnoxious smirk.

"What are *you* doing here?" asked Sam. He didn't remember making any plans for her to come by.

"I brought you this." She held out the submarine book he'd bought at the bookstore. "You left it at my house. I thought you'd want it back."

Sam smiled. "That's what happened to it! I've been looking all over for that." The edge of the cover was torn from where the biker had knocked it right out of his hand, but it was still a book he hadn't read yet. "Thanks!"

The SUV's front window rolled down and Mrs. Murphy waved. "I'll be back in fifteen minutes to get you, Caitlin. I just have to stop at the dry cleaners. Hi, boys!"

"Hey, Mrs. Murphy," answered Sam.

"Okay, Mom," said Caitlin as her mom pulled away.

A door creaked next to them on the cul-de-sac. Sam looked over to see Mr. Haskins flipping through a stack of envelopes in front of his mailbox. "More bills?" he grumbled. "I never buy anything, what are all these bills for?"

"Hi, Mr. Haskins," said Sam.

The old man glanced up and came close to smiling. "How was your bike ride? See any ghosts over on Belle Isle?"

Sam didn't feel like getting into another long conversation with the man. He'd heard enough about ghosts to last him a long time. "Just fine ... no ghosts," he answered.

Derek walked over. "Hey Mr. Haskins, have you ever heard of the Confederate Ghosts? They're some kind of biker gang."

Sam shook his head, wishing Derek hadn't opened his big mouth.

Mr. Haskins turned around with a serious look on his

face. "Now why would you ask a question like that, boy?" He put a hand against his mailbox and shifted his weight.

"Sam had a run-in with them," said Derek, laughing. "Caitlin here actually saved his life."

"I wouldn't go that far," said Sam. He didn't really want to admit to being saved by a girl, even if it was Caitlin.

Caitlin shook her head. "It was the biker's fault. He needs to watch out more for pedestrians."

"Sam usually needs to watch where he's going too," teased Derek.

"What's that now?" asked Mr. Haskins.

Sam tried to think of how to explain. "Well, we were over on Monument Avenue the other day, and a whole bunch of them drove by on their motorcycles. They circled the Robert E. Lee monument in a big parade. They had the Confederate flag on their helmets and bikes, and Caitlin's mom said they were called the Ghosts of the Confederacy."

"It's like your story about the ghosts on Belle Isle," said Derek. "Do you know about them?"

"Now listen," Mr. Haskins said in a serious tone. "Those are some nasty fellas that you need to stay away from. I'm not joking with ya. They're dangerous."

"Who are they?" asked Derek, his ears perking up at the word *danger*.

"Just a group of dirty, no good scoundrels."

"You mean like ne'er-do-wells?" said Sam. That was a word he had learned on another adventure.

"Hmph," cackled Mr. Haskins. "Sure. Whatever you want to call them. They're led by a particularly bad guy named DeWitt. But people call him Mad Dog."

"Mad Dog?" said Caitlin. "What kind of parent names their kid Mad Dog?"

"I'm sure that's not his real name," said Sam.

"Then why do they call him that?" asked Caitlin.

"It's probably a nickname," said Derek. "Just like how we call Sam, Jill."

"Be quiet!" said Sam, faking a punch in Derek's direction.

"Hey, knock it off," barked Mr. Haskins. He leaned closer to them, speaking in a low voice. "Legend goes that he killed a man down in Petersburg over a game of cards."

Yikes.

Sam made a mental note not to play cards with Mad Dog DeWitt.

"Was it Crazy Eights?" asked Derek. "I'm a pro at that game. I bet I could take him."

"Aw, don't worry about that, boy," muttered Mr. Haskins. "You just stay away from those fellas. They'll bring you nothing but trouble."

"Okay," said Sam. It wasn't very hard for him to agree. He didn't *want* to go anywhere near them, although he also didn't imagine he'd ever see them again, either—certainly not if he could help it. He waved the baseball at Derek and motioned to their house. "See ya, Mr. Haskins."

"Don't mention it, boys." Mr. Haskins turned back toward his kitchen door. "And stay off my grass!"

"The Confederate Ghosts," said Caitlin. "They seemed tough. I don't like them, though. They're rude."

"I bet they're cool, riding around on those motorcycles, wind in their hair ..." Derek seemed to drift off into an imaginary world.

"We'll probably never see them again," said Sam.

"I wonder why they were circling General Lee's statue?" asked Caitlin. "They must be paying tribute or something."

Derek threw the ball high into the air and caught it. "I wish I'd been there. I love seeing cool monuments."

"You know where you should go if you want to see more Civil War monuments?" said Caitlin, sitting cross legged on the driveway.

"Washington, D.C.?" said Derek.

"No, Hollywood Cemetery," replied Caitlin.

"Oh, yeah, we're going to Hollywood, baby!" exclaimed Derek. "Now how can we convince Meghan to take us to California before Mom and Dad get home? Maybe Paul can go and Meghan will follow him."

"Actually, she'd probably just call him on the phone," said Sam, turning to Caitlin. "That's all she ever does."

"I'm not talking about California," said Caitlin, shaking her head. "Hollywood Cemetery. It's in Richmond."

"Oh," said Derek with a sigh. "That's not as exciting."

"Isn't that the name of the place in Mr. Haskins' ghost story?" asked Sam, remembering their talk on the porch. "He said the Union soldier ghosts from the island battled the Confederate soldier ghosts from Hollywood Cemetery on the river, or something crazy like that."

"Hmm," said Caitlin. "I don't know about all of that, but you totally should see it. There's thousands of Confederate soldier graves there, plus two U.S. presidents. My parents took me there a couple years ago. Oh, and also Jefferson Davis' grave."

"Wow, that is pretty cool," said Sam, happy to hear about something other than ghosts.

"And one last thing," said Caitlin. "And this is the best one of all."

"Better than Jefferson Davis?" asked Derek, sarcastically. "I don't know if that's possible." He threw another pop fly, his attention seeming to fade.

Caitlin turned to Sam, eager to finish her thought. "There's an enormous monument to the Confederate soldiers that looks like a giant pyramid. It's amazing. I won't tell you any more about it. You'll have to see it for yourself to believe it."

Sam knew that Caitlin got a little overexcited about

history stuff, but a ginormous pyramid did sound pretty sweet. He'd never heard of such a thing in Richmond. "Maybe we can get Meghan to take us to Hollywood after all."

"Where *is* Meghan?" asked Caitlin. "I've still never seen her. It seems like you guys are running around on your own since your parents left."

"Oh, she's inside, probably on the phone with Paul," answered Sam. "She's here though, don't worry."

"Yeah, it's not like we tied her up and locked her in the closet or anything ..." said Derek with an evil grin.

Caitlin looked like she wasn't so sure.

"What?" Derek laughed. "We didn't. I promise."

"Okay," said Caitlin. "When do your parents get home from Europe?"

Sam thought for a moment. "Three days and four hours. But I'm not counting or anything."

A horn honked as Mrs. Murphy's SUV pulled back up to the end of the driveway. "I gotta go," said Caitlin. "Talk to you later. Let me know if you end up going to the cemetery. It's really neat."

"We'll take that under advisement," said Derek.

"Oh, and thanks for the book," called Sam.

CHAPTER TEN

A burning smell greeted Sam at the front door as he walked into the house. He followed his nose to the kitchen and found three mini pizzas smoldering in the toaster oven, small tufts of smoke slipping into the air.

"Meghan!"

"So I told him that I need to be his number one priority. It's a serious thing, you know?" Meghan emerged from the laundry room, her cell phone pressed to her ear. Sam wondered if it was glued there. He didn't know how there could possibly be that much to talk about in a day, but somehow Meghan managed.

Her eyes opened wide at the sight of smoke. "Oh my gosh! Holly, I have to go." She dropped the phone on the counter and dashed over to toaster oven.

"I know, I know," she said, without even looking at Sam. "I told your mom I wasn't a good cook."

Sam doubted that heating up mini pizzas in the toaster oven classified as cooking. If she couldn't do that right, he definitely didn't want to take a chance with real food. He peered down at the round, blackened shapes that Meghan had set on the counter. They were beyond saving. "Was that supposed to be dinner?" he asked, glumly.

"Kind of," said Meghan, looking around the kitchen as if another ready-made meal would suddenly appear out of thin air. "But don't worry, I'll figure something else out."

"Hey, what's for dinner? I'm—" Derek bounded into the kitchen, stopping in mid-sentence on seeing the pizzas. "Oh ... what *was* for dinner?"

Before Meghan could answer, the phone rang in the other room. "I'll get it!" Sam cried.

"If that's your parents," said Meghan, "say nothing about dinner. I'm serious."

Sam sprinted to the phone before Derek could get it. He picked up the cordless from the cradle, pushing the talk button. "Hello?"

"Hi, honey!" Mom's voice answered.

"Hey, Mom!" Sam yelled into the phone. He figured if she was all the way across the ocean, he'd better make sure she could hear him. "How's Paris?"

"Ouch, that's loud, honey. You don't have to yell."

"Oh, sorry. How's Paris?" he repeated in a quieter voice.

"It's amazing! We've had a great time walking around the city and seeing the sights. We're pretty tired though, from the jet lag and all the walking. Did you know it doesn't get dark here until after ten o'clock this time of year?"

Derek nudged Sam, leaning into the phone. "Put it on speaker. I want to hear."

Sam pushed another button.

"Hi, Mom! Did you see the Eiffel Tower?" asked Derek.

Mom laughed. "Yes we did. It was beautiful. And we've been to three different museums and some incredible dinners. How are you guys doing with Meghan? We miss you!"

"We're trying to keep her in line," answered Derek, smiling.

"Is she feeding you okay?"

Sam looked toward the kitchen, remembering the burnt pizza. "It's been sizzling!"

"Are you behaving yourselves?"

"Mom, can you imagine us not behaving?" said Derek. "Meghan has barely noticed us."

Sam tried to hold in a laugh.

"Oh, I'm sure. Here, Dad wants to say hi."

"Hey, guys!"

"Hi, Dad," the boys echoed. "See anything cool?"

"Well, does a soccer match count as cool?" answered Dad.

"No way!" exclaimed Derek. "That's awesome. Are you serious?"

"Yep. Don't worry, I just may have gotten you a jersey. If we get a good report from Meghan, that is."

"All right! Thanks, Dad. I can't wait to see it," said Derek, pumping his fist.

"Did you get me anything?" Sam asked hopefully.

"Oh, sorry, honey, did you want something too?" said Mom. "We totally forgot!"

"Mom!"

"I'm just kidding," she said with a laugh. "We might keep your gift a surprise. You'll have to wait until we get home."

Sam sighed in relief. "Which is soon, right?"

"Not long. Don't worry," Dad answered. "We love you guys."

"We love you, too," said Sam.

"Can I talk to Meghan?" Mom asked.

"Sure, I'll get her. I think she's done talking to the fireman by now." Derek pulled the phone out of Sam's hand and walked toward the kitchen. "Meghan! Mom wants to know how dinner's going!"

Sam grimaced at Derek's joke. Even though Meghan

mostly left them alone, she could be tough and little bit mean. There was still more than enough time left for her to make their lives miserable. He leaned back on the couch. He felt his eyes tearing up, but wiped them away before Derek came back in the room. He didn't want Derek to see him crying. Hearing his parents' voices suddenly made him realize how much he missed them.

He tried to shift his thoughts to something else, remembering what Caitlin had said about Hollywood Cemetery. The big pyramid sounded cool, but he hated graveyards. Maybe they'd ask Meghan to take them there tomorrow, if she didn't burn the house down.

Derek and Meghan walked back into the room. "Okay, get your shoes on," said Meghan. "We're eating out."

Derek leaned over to Sam. "I think she's in trouble."

Sam smiled weakly and headed for the door. "Meghan, have you ever been to Hollywood?"

CHAPTER ELEVEN

A light drizzle was falling as the boys walked down through the metal gates to Hollywood Cemetery the next morning. It hadn't been too hard to convince Meghan to take them once she'd realized it was near Paul's office.

Sam knew his parents wouldn't approve of so much free rein. He had talked about it with Derek, but they'd decided that if anyone was going to get in trouble, it would be Meghan. Maybe that wasn't a good attitude, but it did give them a chance to explore.

"What's the worst that can happen?" Derek had said. But Sam had been on enough of their adventures to know they could get into a lot of trouble on their own. Things usually worked out okay in the end, but he wasn't entirely sure if it was due to their good luck or their skill at solving mysteries. He suspected that the longer he went along with Derek and his crazy schemes, the sooner their luck was destined to run out.

A thick fog settled across the cemetery, making it hard to see farther than a hundred feet in front of them. Roads and pathways stretched out in every direction with grassy sections in between, jam-packed with old, graying, stone grave markers and larger, above-ground crypts.

They'd both walked through a cemetery before at St. John's Church, but that was nothing compared to this place. It was like comparing a sandbox to the beach. This was mammoth! Everything was eerily quiet—birds weren't singing, traffic couldn't be heard. Maybe the fog was absorbing all the sound, like a black hole, or maybe it was just always quiet and sad at a cemetery.

Every now and then, they'd stop to look at a stone and read a date. "I wish we had a map," said Sam, looking at the sections of graves that seemed to stretch on forever. "How are we going to find the pyramid? All these paths look the same." He was determined to find the monument to the Confederate soldiers and the presidents' graves that Caitlin had told them about.

"Meghan's picking us up at noon," said Derek. "That means we still have an hour."

"But we haven't seen anything yet. Where is all the good stuff?"

"How about up there?" Derek pointed to a section, separated from the rest of the tombstones by an important looking, circular path. "I don't think we've gone that way yet."

They raced up the path to the new section. Statues of angels covered several graves that formed a circle around a larger bronze statue of a man in a long coat with a hat in his hand.

Derek read a plaque below the statue. "Jefferson Davis!"

That was one of the graves that Caitlin had told them about—the president of the Confederate States. Sam studied the plaque on the stone pedestal under the statue.

"It says that besides being the Confederate president, Davis was also the secretary of war, and a senator from Mississippi. That's impressive!"

"Let's keep walking," said Derek. "I think I can see the river over there." They continued down the path to another unique-looking cluster of graves. The first resembled a large metal prison cell, except it was extra fancy and elegant.

"Who is that?" asked Sam, pointing to the grave.

"James Monroe, fifth president of the United States," read Derek. "Cool."

"And look over there, I think that's another special one." Sam rushed over to a large, pointed stone with a sculpture of a head. "John Tyler, President of the United States, 1841 to 1845."

Derek whistled. "Man, this place has more presidents than Washington, D.C."

"Except that all of these are dead," said Sam.

A loud whistle pulled their attention down the hill and straight across the valley to the James River.

"Whoa, check out that view!" exclaimed Derek.

Sam stretched his neck for a better view. "I don't get it, where's the train? We heard the whistle."

Another blast rang out through the valley.

Sam covered his ears. "It sounds like it's right on top of us, but I don't see it!"

"That's because *we're* on top of *it*!" Derek hollered, pointing down the hill. They moved a few steps closer to the crest of the hill. At the bottom of the incline, a train track slipped between them and the river. A long freight train chugged slowly but steadily along. It pulled cars with all types of containers—open cargo cars with coal, black rounded tanker cars, and square box cars with racks of fluffy, white-feathered chickens.

"Think we can hop on and catch a ride to Vegas?" Derek shouted over the din. "We could be stowaways."

"Sure, go ahead," answered Sam. "You can ride in the chicken car. I'll see you later."

Derek punched Sam in the arm good-naturedly as they watched the train gradually move around the bend, its metallic roar fading into the distance. They could see better now that the fog had lifted. The tall buildings of downtown Richmond rose to their left. He looked across the river at a familiar-looking bridge. "Is that the bridge we walked across to get to Belle Isle?" He was sure he recognized the suspended bridge.

"Where?" Derek squinted into the glare of the sun.

"Right over there. Next to where that single stone pillar is standing out of the rapids."

"Hey, you're right. That is the bridge. I wonder if we can see the hydro plant from here? That place was cool. We should go back there before Mom and Dad get home."

"I think I saw enough while we were there," muttered Sam, remembering the ghost painting on the wall and the men's voices. "Besides, I don't want to run into Cameron and his buddies again on the trail, do you?"

"They'll be gone, don't worry about them, Sam. I can handle it." Derek put a tough face, but Sam detected a glimmer of concern.

Sam reached down and scratched the knee that was starting to scab over. "Maybe if we stick to the main loop."

"You can stick to the kindergarten loop," said Derek, suddenly acting annoyed. "I want to hit those steep trails again. They're not that hard. You just have to watch where you're going."

"It wasn't my fault that those guys pulled out in front

of me," argued Sam. "The same thing could have happened to you if they'd come by sooner."

"Yeah, but it didn't," said Derek.

"You were lucky."

"It's skill, Sam, not luck. Try and be tough for once in your life." Derek turned away from the river, bumping into Sam with a shove as he walked back to the trail.

Because the boys were bickering, they didn't notice a noise growing louder in the cemetery. It wasn't the deep rumble of the train, but a low hum moving closer by the second. Sam finally heard it and spun around, staring at the crest of the hill. He recognized that sound. Suddenly a motorcycle emerged from the tree line. Then another, and another.

"Quick, get behind the tombstones!" yelled Derek.

Sam's heart leaped into his throat. "Is it the Confederate Ghosts?"

"How should I know, Sam? Just hide!"

CHAPTER TWELVE

The boys scrambled behind the nearest grave marker, crouching down low as the roar of the bikes grew louder. Soon, more than a dozen motorcycles passed by on the nearest paved path. Sam immediately recognized the Confederate flag on the helmet of the lead bike. It was the same as the one he had seen on Monument Avenue.

Mad Dog DeWitt.

He swallowed hard, remembering Mr. Haskins' story. What were the Confederate Ghosts doing in the cemetery? The bikes slowed to a stop when they reached the circle path around Jefferson Davis' grave.

"Are those the bikers you saw with Caitlin?" asked Derek.

"Yeah, that's them. The guy in the lead with the tattoos must be Mad Dog. He's the one that almost ran me over. Look where they stopped—right at Jefferson Davis' grave. What do you think they're doing?"

"There's only one way to find out," said Derek, inching forward in a half-crouch. "You stay here. It's probably too scary for you." He burst away from the gravestone in the direction of the bikers.

"Derek, wait!" hissed Sam, but his brother was already gone. Sam sat there for a few more beats, watching Derek sneak farther up the grass, moving stealthily from stone to stone. "This is ridiculous," Sam muttered, sinking down in the thick grass, crawling one arm at a time like a soldier.

Derek impatiently waved him over to the crypt he was hiding behind. Sam dove next to him, breathing hard.

"Try to keep it down, Sam! You don't know the first thing about being inconspicuous. Why couldn't you just stay back there?"

Sam tried to catch his breath. "What are you doing? These guys are a biker gang. You heard Mr. Haskins, they're dangerous."

"Just be quiet and stay down," said Derek. "They're having some kind of a meeting, or a ceremony, or something."

Sam peered over the crypt at the men. They'd placed themselves in a circle around the Jefferson Davis monu-ment, standing an equal distance from each other, bikes parked behind them. Two of the men stood off to the side, like sentries on their post, ensuring that no one wandered in.

One man moved forward. It was Mad Dog. He stood in front of the grave, clasped his hands at his waist, with his head down. Was he praying? This was weird. "What's he doing?"

"Shh!" said Derek, waving at Sam to stay back.

Suddenly the man lifted his head, looking around the cemetery like he'd heard something. Sam held his breath. After a moment, Mad Dog reached behind the lower part of the statue, like he was touching Davis' shoe. What was he doing?

Then Mad Dog stepped away, only to have his odd actions repeated by the others. One by one, they all moved up to the statue, bowed their heads, and reached behind the foot of the statue.

"Oh my gosh," whispered Sam. "I bet its some kind of weird ritual. They probably kidnap lost kids to use as human sacrifices."

Derek frowned and smacked Sam's shoulder. "Shut up. Who are they going to sacrifice us to, Jefferson Davis? That doesn't make any sense. He's already dead."

"Doesn't it? Or does it make so much sense that you can't even imagine it?!" said Sam, eyes bulging.

When the last of the bikers had paid their strange respects to Jefferson Davis' foot, the gang remounted their bikes. Mad Dog started his engine, driving slowly around the circle and directly toward the boys' hiding spot.

"Get down!" said Derek, dropping flat in the grass behind the crypt.

They could hear the loud engines of the motorcycles roaring to life. Only after they'd passed by did they poke their heads past the side of the stone crypt. Sam's heart was still racing as he watched Mad Dog gently turn out into the cemetery. One by one, the bikes rounded the path in a solemn parade. It reminded Sam of the scenes he'd viewed on TV where police or firefighters paid tribute to their fallen colleagues.

When the last of the motorcycles had disappeared down the hill, the two sentinels boarded their bikes and took up the rear. Sam looked again at one of their jackets and gasped.

"What is it?" asked Derek, as the motors gradually faded out of earshot.

"A ghost …" answered Sam.

"Right, Sam, we already know they are called the Confederate Ghosts. Hello?" Derek sighed in frustration as he stood up from behind the crypt. He looked cautiously back and forth, then headed toward the Jefferson Davis statue.

Sam wondered why Derek was getting so annoyed with him. This was serious business, not just his imagination. He knew neither of them wanted to get caught by the bikers, but ever since Sam had brought up Cameron at the river, Derek seemed in a bad mood. Which sort of made sense, but Derek didn't need to take his frustrations out on him!

"See anything?" Sam asked, scanning the area for lurking sentinels.

Derek was leaning over the statue's pedestal, inspecting the area around Jefferson Davis' shoe where the men had been focused. "Look at that!" Derek pointed at two small letters, scribbled in a black chalk-like substance. Next to the letters was a thick red line, pressed onto the stone like it had been drawn on top of itself over and over again.

"*CG*," read Sam. "Confederate Ghosts?"

"Yep, but look at the lines next to it."

"Is that red marker?" asked Sam.

Derek leaned closer. He put his nose up to the stone and sniffed, shaking his head. "It's not marker … it's blood."

Sam leaped back from the statue. "Blood! Holy cow. This is bad. This is very bad. I told you we shouldn't be here. I told you they were going to do sacrifices."

"Relax, Sam. It's not *your* blood."

"Not yet, it's not, but I bet they'll want it to be once they find out we're from the North."

Derek rolled his eyes and looked back at the statue.

"Sacrifices. I told you!" bawled Sam. "Sacrifices to their old president, with Union blood from Northern kids."

Derek ignored Sam and walked around the perimeter of Davis' grave area looking for clues.

"What I was trying to tell you before you stormed off, was about what was on the guy's jacket," said Sam, following behind.

"Okay, Sam, what was on his jacket?"

"A ghost! Exactly like the mural at the hydro plant on Belle Isle. He had the same picture of the ghost outlined on his jacket!"

Derek finally stopped walking around the statue. "Are you sure?"

"Positive. I'd remember that drawing anywhere," said Sam, looking back at the red marks on the statue. "We need to get out of here. Meghan's going to pick us up soon, and we still have to find our way back to the entrance."

Sam looked around nervously at the graveyard. He was surrounded by the dead and he didn't want to join them.

Derek looked at his watch. "Okay, let's go."

"Thank you. That's the smartest thing you've said all morning."

"Just try to keep it together, Sam. Don't be such a baby."

"Shut up, I'm not a baby. You can stop being such a jerk. Just because I mentioned Cameron—"

"And keep an eye out for the bikers," interrupted Derek. "They should be gone by now, but I don't want to sneak up on them accidentally."

Don't worry, thought Sam. I'm on high alert.

They did their best to retrace their steps to the entrance, but it was hard to follow the twists and turns. They didn't see any more bikers, but they were lost.

"These roads all look the same," said Sam, wiping the sweat off his brow. It was getting warmer the longer they were in the cemetery.

"Let's take a break," said Derek. "I need to get our bearings."

Sam looked across the path at an especially elaborate grave that reminded him of a tower. Derek must have been looking at the same thing.

"Do you think Mom and Dad are climbing the Eiffel Tower right now?"

"They said they already saw it," replied Sam.

"I hope they bring me a snow globe."

"A snow globe of what?"

"Of the Eiffel Tower, duh," said Derek.

"Do they even have snow globes with the Eiffel Tower in them? I don't think it snows in Paris."

"Sure they do," answered Derek. "They make snow globes of everything. Mark Perkins told me that his cousin went to Egypt and brought him back a snow globe of the pyramids."

"That's crazy."

"Everybody loves snow globes."

"Hmm," muttered Sam. He didn't want a snow globe. He didn't like to think about their mom and dad climbing the Eiffel Tower, either. It was high. Too high.

He thought back to the time that he'd climbed to the top of a lighthouse with his dad at the beach. It had seemed like a great idea from the ground, with his neck craned back into his shoulder, watching the tiny people at the top. But once he got inside, he started to change his mind. The iron staircase wound around the old lighthouse's walls, seeming to stretch up to eternity. The more steps they took, the more Sam wanted to get back on the ground. It was terrible.

"Sam, come on!" Derek hollered, pulling him out of his daydream. Sam sighed and followed, turning yet another corner filled with rows of short, white, rounded grave markers. Just when it seemed like nothing would ever look different, a dark shadow emerged from behind the trees. As his eyes moved upwards, Sam's mouth dropped open in amazement. "What is that?"

CHAPTER THIRTEEN

"Whoa ..." said Derek.

"It's huge!" cried Sam, walking forward, his head leaned back.

"It's like an Egyptian pyramid," said Derek. "Except gray instead of brown."

This was definitely the monument Caitlin had told them about. Sam had forgotten all about it after their run-in with the bikers. Now he understood why she had made such a big deal about it.

"I wonder if they make a snow globe of *this*?" Derek laughed.

Sam chuckled, marveling at the enormous pyramid of rocks. It wasn't just a pile of stones stacked on top of each other, but more like a building constructed in the shape of a pyramid.

"Well, I guess we found the Confederate soldiers monument," said Derek.

"I never expected it to be so big!" Sam exclaimed. The rocks were huge, rectangular stones, each one of them three feet tall. The whole thing was bigger than his house! As they moved around the pyramid, Sam spied an inscription on one of the lower stones.

TO THE CONFEDERATE DEAD.

He thought about what that meant—how thousands of men who had died fighting for what they believed in were buried in the ground here.

He walked around to the next side and saw another plaque.

ERECTED BY THE HOLLY-WOOD MEMORIAL ASSOCIATION. A.D. 1869.

Sam raised his eyebrow and turned to his brother. "1869 was over a hundred years ago. How could they have built this? There weren't any cranes and forklifts back then, were there?"

"I don't think so," said Derek. "Maybe it was the ghosts."

"The bikers?" asked Sam. "I don't think they built it."

"No, the *real* ghosts, of the dead Confederate soldiers

that Mr. Haskins told us about." Derek lowered his voice to a hushed tone as if someone might overhear. "What he didn't say was that each night, after the Confederate soldiers rose from their graves and battled the Union soldiers, they dragged a stone back from the river. One by one, they heaved stone after stone onto the pyramid, stacking it higher and higher."

"Give me a break," said Sam, shaking his head. He'd heard this kind of nonsense from his brother too many times.

"For over a hundred years," Derek continued, keeping a serious face, "the Confederate Ghosts have served as the protectors of this monument to the dead. In the early days, they rode on all black horses. Today, they ride on Harleys. But their mission is the same."

"And what's that?" said Sam, laughing now at Derek's tall tale. "To touch the shoe of Jefferson Davis' statue?"

"No, to recommit themselves to the Confederate cause through a streak of their blood, which shall forever remain true to the South."

"Right ..." said Sam.

"Oh, I forgot the most important part! Each night, since the pyramid was assembled, the statue of Jefferson Davis comes to life."

"Oh," Sam laughed. "And I assume he's joined by General Robert E. Lee on horseback too."

"Exactly!" said Derek, jumping into the air, his arm

slashing back and forth with a pretend sword. "Together they fight all night, until the rising sun chases them back into their graves at dawn."

Sam shook his head. "That's all very interesting, but let's get going. Meghan's going to be here any minute, and we still don't know where the entrance is. She's going to be mad if we're not there."

"Good point," said Derek. "The only thing worse than facing an angry Confederate Ghost might be an angry Meghan. Let's go."

They gave the pyramid one more appreciative look before scampering down the road. Somehow, they made the right combination of turns, and soon they recognized the path to the entrance.

"Look, there she is," said Derek, pointing to the parked minivan.

"Where have you guys been?" yelled Meghan, opening the doors. "Come on, let's go."

"Where are we going?" asked Sam as he buckled his seat belt.

"Well," said Meghan, "Derek has *another* soccer practice at two o'clock." She turned to Sam. "And your little friend Caitlin called while you were out and asked if you wanted to come by the bookstore again this afternoon. If not, I'll have to take you back home."

Derek elbowed Sam in the ribs and winked, mouthing the word *cuddle*, with a laugh.

Sam smacked him in the arm. "Shut up."

"I need to meet Paul at the pool," continued Meghan, "so hurry up and let me know what you want to do. I didn't sign up to be your personal secretary."

"Didn't you just see Paul this morning?" asked Derek.

"That's not any of your business," snapped Meghan.

Sam wiped the sweat from his forehead. The pool sounded nice and refreshing after the cemetery.

"Can I bring Caitlin to the pool?" he asked. They didn't have to hang out with Meghan and Paul while they were there. Besides, he wanted to tell Caitlin about all they'd seen at the cemetery.

Meghan let out an exaggerated sigh. "Sure, why not. What's one more rug rat to cart around. I can't believe your parents won't be home for two more days."

"One and a half, actually," corrected Sam.

"Whatever." Meghan handed her cell phone to Sam over the seat back. "Here, why don't you call her and ask if she wants to come to the pool. Her mom's number is in there."

Sam took the phone and started pushing buttons to find Mrs. Murphy's number when the phone came to life with a buzz. The word *Paul* flashed on the screen.

"Um, I think you're getting a phone call," said Sam.

"Well, give it to me then, will you?" said Meghan.

"You're driving. That's not safe," said Derek. "Here, I'll answer it." He grabbed the phone from Sam's hand

and pressed the *Speaker* button. "Paul, buddy, what's happening?"

A deep voice on the other end of the line answered, "Hello?"

"Will you give me that phone, Derek?" said Meghan from the front seat. She turned her head to reach backwards, causing the car to veer sharply to the right.

"Watch out, Meghan," yelled Sam. "You're going to kill us!"

Meghan straightened back in her seat, yanking the wheel to the left. A car in the next lane honked and sped ahead of them.

"Meghan, are you there?" asked Paul, still waiting on the phone.

"Paul, this is Derek. Meghan is a little busy trying to kill us by driving down the middle of the road. What's cooking?" He looked up at Meghan with a grimace. "Sorry, I didn't mean to bring up a sensitive subject."

Sam shook his head. Derek loved to talk like a big shot, especially on the phone.

Meghan yelled from the front seat. "Honey, I have to run these little creeps a hundred more places before I can meet you at the pool. I'm going to be late." She seemed more annoyed than ever.

Sam pictured her dropping them off on the side of the road somewhere and making them walk home. He wouldn't put it past her.

"That's no problem," said Paul through the phone. "I'm still tied up over here at the bike shop. We got a new shipment of Cannondales in this morning that I need to set up. I won't be able to get to the pool until three. See you then?"

"Okay. Miss you like crazy!"

"Miss you too, kitten. Thanks for stopping by this morning. Bye."

"Bye."

Sam and Derek looked at each other and burst out laughing. What was that all about? The name *kitten* just didn't seem to fit Meghan. Maybe *mountain lion* would be more appropriate.

"Not a word," warned Meghan, sensing the boys' thoughts. "Sam, hurry up and make your phone call or the only part of the pool you'll be visiting is the bottom of the deep end."

Sam wiped the smile from his face and started dialing. She looked like she meant it.

Yikes.

CHAPTER FOURTEEN

"Ah, this is the life," sighed Sam from his lounge chair, his head propped on a folded towel. After dropping Derek off at soccer practice, they'd picked Caitlin up at her house and headed to the pool.

"I like helping at the bookstore, but I have to admit, this *is* better right now," said Caitlin, flipping through a book she'd brought along. She was always reading something. Sam guessed that was how she always knew so much. He was getting there, but he was still way behind her.

"Is this the pool you come to for swim team?" asked Sam.

"No, that's the one in Julie Mercer's neighborhood. We're the *Silver Minnows*. I came in third place for the backstroke in our last meet. I was hoping for first, but Julie and this really fast girl from the other team beat me.

Mom says third place is still good, but I was disappointed."

Sam had never been on the swim team. He'd played plenty of baseball and basketball, but his teams never seemed to win much. Last year, Derek's baseball team went all the way to the county pennant game. Derek even hit a home run, but they ended up losing in the last inning. "Third place is good. I'm not the best player on my baseball team either. I really want to start at short-stop, but I keep getting stuck in left field."

"Is left field bad?"

"Not necessarily—one of my favorite players on the Yankees plays left field—but in Little League, it doesn't get a lot of action. Not that many kids can hit the ball to the outfield yet, so it's kind of boring. I'd rather play shortstop."

"Well, I'll bet you're working at it and getting better," said Caitlin, encouragingly. "Just like in school. You don't give up—you're always trying to study harder if you get a bad grade on a math test."

Sam considered what Caitlin said. He'd never really thought about whether he was persistent like that; but now that she said it, he realized it was true. His mom had always said that girls are very observant.

"Hey, look who it is! Little Jackson!" a voice screeched over at them. Sam closed his eyes, hoping that it wasn't who he thought it was.

"How's your bike, Little Jackson?" another voice asked, coming closer.

Sam opened his eyes and saw Cameron and one of his buddies from Belle Isle walking up.

"Look, Sean, he has a girlfriend. What's your name, sweetheart?" asked Cameron.

The other boy, Sean, erupted in an obnoxious high-pitched laugh that sounded like a hyena.

Sam waved his hand weakly. "Hi, guys, I'm fine, thanks."

"Where's your chicken brother? Staying home for the rest of the summer with his mommy?" Sean nudged Cameron in the side, bending over with his hyena laugh again like he'd said something really hilarious.

Caitlin stood up, setting her book on her towel "I'm getting hot. Let's go down the waterslide, Sam."

Sam hopped up from his chair. The waterslide sounded good to him. Anything would be better than talking to Cameron and Sean.

"Okay, see you later, Sammy," called Cameron. "Be careful on your bike. Maybe you should try some training wheels next time."

"They're such jerks," Sam muttered as he walked to the waterslide with Caitlin. "Those are the guys we saw on Belle Isle when I cut my arm."

"Yeah, I figured that out," said Caitlin. "Just ignore them. That's what my dad says to do with bullies. They're just trying to make themselves seem cool by putting everyone else down."

Sam nodded, but knew her suggestion was easier said than done.

* * *

FROM THE TOP of the waterslide, Sam could see his lounge chair, the snack bar, and Meghan and Paul, sitting next to the deep-water pool. They were holding hands and listening to music on their phones. There was no sign of Cameron—he must have found someone else to bother.

The waterslide wasn't huge, like at an amusement park, but it was pretty impressive for a local pool. At the top, two tubes ran side by side, spiraling in tight curves to the bottom. They shot the rider out three feet above the water so that they exploded into the air, falling into a big splash. It was fun—a little scary the first time Sam had tried it—but now he liked it.

"Sure you're ready for the hurricane?" he asked Caitlin, stepping up to the slide.

"Oh, I'm ready. Prepare to eat my dust," said Caitlin, laughing. "On the count of three." Sam put his hands on the bar above his red tube for extra momentum on the push off. He readied himself for Caitlin's count from the yellow tube next to his.

"One … two …"

Sam tightened his grip on the bar.

"Go!" Caitlin yelled, shooting forward into her slide.

What? That wasn't fair! She didn't say three! Sam dropped awkwardly into his tube without any momentum. "Caitliiiiin!" he yelled, building speed through the tube. He could hear her screams through the other tube as they flew around the curves.

Sam burst out the bottom, arms waving as he splashed into the water. Caitlin was already paddling toward the side of the pool ahead of him. He wiped the water from his eyes and kicked his way to the wall. "You cheated!"

"What are you talking about? You didn't hear me say three?" Caitlin giggled. "I warned you that you couldn't keep up with a girl!"

"Whatever," said Sam. "You know you cheated. You're worse than Derek."

"Oh, now I'm really insulted!"

After a few more rides down the slide, they dried off with their towels and headed to the deep pool.

"Be careful," said Sam. "Meghan and Paul are over here." He a gagging face.

They sat on the concrete side of the large rectangular pool, legs hanging in the water. Half the pool had plastic ropes that marked swimming lanes under small diving platforms for races. On the side where they were sitting, the pool was open with the depth marked *8 FT* in blue paint. It was far too deep for Sam to stand, but he'd been working on treading water, and he knew he could swim there as long as he didn't go too far from the side. Just in case, he glanced up at the lifeguard across the pool. She was swinging a whistle around in a circle, but seemed to be paying attention.

Sam waved weakly to Meghan. She looked right at him but didn't wave back. She had on reflective sunglasses so he couldn't see her eyes and was turned in her lounge chair so that Paul could rub sunscreen on her back.

Paul was different than Sam had expected. He looked like a tight end on the New York Giants, but was surprisingly nice. That didn't seem to fit with what Sam knew of Meghan. Maybe she was nice to everyone but them.

"So how was Hollywood Cemetery?" asked Caitlin, kicking small waves of water from the edge.

Sam told her about seeing the Confederate monument, the graves of the presidents, and then about the bikers.

"Wow," said Caitlin. "What do you think they were doing there?"

Sam frowned. "I don't want to know. I told Derek that if they find out we're Yankees from the North, they'll kill us."

"I'll protect you, Sam," Caitlin said, laughing as she slapped him on the shoulder.

He hadn't been expecting the push, and slipped off the edge of the wall with a splash. He swam back to the surface, coughing water out of his lungs. "What the heck?"

"Whoops. Sorry. Are you okay?"

Sam pretended to be angry. "If that's you protecting me, I think I'll be better off without you!"

Caitlin smiled as Sam climbed out of the water. "Do you really think they put a mark on the statue in blood? That's pretty weird."

Sam wiped water from his face. "Who knows? That's what Derek said, but he might have been messing with me. Whatever they were doing, it was not good."

Caitlin stood up. "Move back and watch this." She turned around, placing her heels right on the edge. "Prepare to be amazed!"

Before Sam could ask what she was doing, Caitlin bent her knees and jumped backwards in the air, arching her back and gracefully slipping into the water with hardly a splash.

Sam watched in surprise while Caitlin kicked back to the surface. Her head popped above the water, a huge smile on her face.

"Ta-da!"

"Wow!" said Sam. "I *am* amazed. That was sweet! What was it?"

"That was my back dive. I've been practicing it at swim team."

Caitlin was full of surprises. Sam had known she was smart, but had never realized she was such a good swimmer. He tried to remember how she bent her back in the air like that. He feared that his spine would snap in half if he tried it.

A whistle blew from the lifeguard stand, signaling that it would be adult swim time for the next ten minutes, so Caitlin and Sam bought treats at the snack bar.

"Nice and refreshing," said Sam, his rainbow snow cone crunching in his teeth. They had brought their treats to the chairs next to Meghan. They all watched Paul swim laps.

"Is he in the Olympics or something?" asked Caitlin.

"I don't know, but he motors through the water like a speed boat." Sam took another bite of his snow cone. "Do you think they had *Icees* back in the Civil War?"

Caitlin laughed. "I doubt it. I don't think they even had freezers back then."

"Ice houses."

Sam looked up, surprised to see that it was Meghan who had spoken. "What?"

"Ice houses. That's what they used instead of freezers," she repeated.

Sam thought about it for a second. That didn't make

any sense at all. "Why would they build houses out of ice? And how would you even know that, Meghan?"

"I'm studying American history."

"You *are*?" said Sam, in disbelief. He couldn't picture Meghan doing anything overly intelligent, but she *was* in college. If she didn't get a job from studying history, maybe when she graduated she could be a prison guard.

"Wow, that's super cool," said Caitlin. "You probably know a lot about what Sam and I have been talking about then." She nudged Sam.

"Um ..." Sam tried to think of a question. He was sure he had a lot of them. "So ... what happened to General Lee after he left Richmond?" There, that was a pretty good question.

"Seriously?" Meghan sighed, peering over the top of her sunglasses as if Sam's question was way too basic.

"Don't you know the answer?" said Sam.

Meghan sat up straight in her lounge chair. "Well, once Lee and his troops evacuated Richmond, they moved west of here to Appomattox Courthouse. They'd hoped to connect with another part of the Confederate Army, but it didn't work. So he surrendered to General Grant at Appomattox."

Sam remembered Mr. Haskins saying something about Appomattox. "He gave up?" That wasn't what he'd expected from the famous General Lee.

"Sam," said Caitlin, "you do know the North won the war, don't you?"

"Yeah, but it sounded like Lee was such a great general. I didn't think he'd be the one to surrender."

Meghan raised her eyebrows. "Lee wanted to end the casualties. He really had little choice but to surrender."

Sam scrunched his face, trying to remember what casualties meant.

"That's the number of soldiers killed," Caitlin whispered, seeming to read his thoughts.

"Sometimes the greatest leaders know when to give up," said Meghan. "Lee had seen enough bloodshed. Four long years of war had resulted in over 600,000 dead. Although, there were actually more Union casualties than Confederate."

"That's terrible," said Sam. "It's a good thing he surrendered then, I guess."

"You two should go to the Civil War museum at Tredegar. That way I don't have to be your encyclopedia."

"That's right next to Belle Isle where we rode our bikes," said Sam. "Why didn't you say something when you dropped us off the other morning?"

"How was I to know you were a history buff?" said Meghan, "I just thought you wanted to ride bikes."

"Maybe we can go tomorrow?" suggested Caitlin. "My mom can take us. It's not that far from the bookstore. Do you think Derek would want to come?"

"Maybe. We can ask him," said Sam. "Is that okay, Meghan?"

"Works for me. The less time I have to watch you two the better."

"Isn't that your *job*, to watch us while Mom and Dad are away?" asked Sam. He'd been thinking it all week, and it was about time someone said it. "They're paying you, aren't they?"

"I'm watching you now, aren't I?" said Meghan.

The whistle blew again, and kids started jumping back into the pool. "Let's go," said Sam, hopping out of his chair.

"She's not very nice, is she?" asked Caitlin. "Why did your parents leave you with her?"

"Well," answered Sam, sliding back into the water, "she *is* our cousin, so I think they must trust her. And it's only for a few days. It could be worse."

"How could it be worse?"

"We could be *Paul!*" said Sam, laughing. He made a silly kissing face before diving under the water.

CHAPTER FIFTEEN

"I s this going to be a boring museum?" Derek moaned from the back seat of Mrs. Murphy's car. He hadn't been overly excited when Sam had told him they were going to the Civil War museum with Caitlin and her mom.

Meghan had said he didn't have a choice, however, since she was spending the day with Paul. Derek said it was going on his list of complaints to Mom and Dad. But then Meghan asked him if he'd like to walk to soccer practice. She was tough.

"Now what kind of attitude is that?" Mrs. Murphy asked Derek from the driver's seat. "I've never seen a museum that was boring, only bad attitudes from the visitors."

"Get ready to be surprised," mumbled Derek, staring out the window.

Caitlin turned to Sam. "Mom used to be a teacher. That's how she knows so many things. She thinks I'd be a good teacher someday too. What do you think?"

"Sure," said Sam. She acted like the teacher in class half the time already, so it was probably true. He thought about the museum. "There's something I don't get about the Civil War."

"Just one thing?" Mrs. Murphy laughed. "You're doing pretty well if that's all. The war was a complicated time. There's a lot that folks don't understand."

Sam nodded. "What I mean is, how come there isn't a statue on Monument Avenue for Abraham Lincoln? He was the president, wasn't he?"

"That's a good observation, Sam," said Mrs. Murphy.

"He's very observant," said Derek.

"We didn't see a monument, because there isn't one," said Mrs. Murphy as the car turned off the highway.

"But how could there not be a statue of Lincoln?" asked Sam. "He was the president who freed the slaves, right? That seems worthy of a monument to me."

"Yes, he was the president, and he signed the Emancipation Proclamation, which officially ended slavery," said Mrs. Murphy.

"Then why isn't there a statue?" Caitlin's mom seemed to know her stuff, but maybe she was wrong about this one.

"Well, it likely has something to do with the fact that

Richmond was part of the Confederacy that was defeated by the Union Army."

"But it *was* a good thing to end slavery," said Caitlin.

"Of course, honey," said Mrs. Murphy, "but no matter how good the end of the war may have been in the long run, many people in the South were not too happy about it at the time. Setting up a statue of the leader of the opposition was a little too much to ask."

"Kind of like putting up a statue of Mickey Mantle in Fenway Park," said Derek.

"Sure, kind of like that," Mrs. Murphy laughed.

"Except a lot more important, Derek," said Caitlin.

"Tell that to a Red Sox fan."

The car turned into the museum parking lot, and everyone piled out. Derek pointed across the river. "Look, there's Belle Isle."

Sam saw the suspension bridge and thought again about the mural in the hydro plant. He wondered if there were any Confederate Ghost bikers at the hideout right now. He tried to shake those thoughts from his mind and turned back to the building they were walking toward. "Where's the museum? All I see is that old factory."

"That *is* the museum, Sam. Duh," said Caitlin, following her mom along the sidewalk. "It's built into the old metal factory they used during the Civil War."

"Whoa, look at the cannon!" yelled Derek, running

over to a big metal gun that guarded the building. He stood behind it, pretending to aim at Sam's head.

Mrs. Murphy stopped when they reached the front door. "You know, Sam, I forgot to mention that there *is* one statue of Lincoln in Richmond."

"Aha!" exclaimed Sam. He knew there had to be one. "It's probably huge, right? Is it at the state capitol building?"

"No, it's actually right here, at the museum."

"It is?" Sam glanced around but didn't see anything.

"Yep, see if you can find it."

"That shouldn't be too hard. I'll bet it's in a big display," said Sam.

Derek ran past. "Ten points to whoever sees it first, Sam."

"You guys are always competing about something," sighed Caitlin. "Why don't you look around and try to actually learn something?"

"That's why we have you around," shouted Derek, bolting into the lobby.

"Wait up!" yelled Sam, chasing Derek through the doors.

Caitlin turned to her mom and shook her head slowly. "Boys!"

* * *

AFTER AN HOUR of walking through the museum, Sam felt like he'd seen almost all there was to see. He'd viewed dozens of soldier uniforms, weapons, and maps of the different battles, but couldn't find anything close to a statue of Abraham Lincoln.

Mrs. Murphy and Caitlin were reading an illuminated map depicting General Lee's march to Appomattox when the boys walked up to her with discouraged faces. "Okay, we give up," said Sam.

"We can't find the statue anywhere," said Derek. "Where is it?"

Mrs. Murphy looked up from the map. "Why don't you go out behind the museum and see if you find anything."

"Outside?" said Derek. "Why didn't you tell us that in the first place?"

"Because I wanted you to see the rest of the museum, of course," said Mrs. Murphy, smiling.

"Oh," moaned Derek. "Thanks a lot."

"Anytime, boys!"

Sam was the first out the door. He scanned the grassy hill all the way to the parking lot for a huge monument honoring the former president, but he didn't see anything.

"Look! I found it!" Caitlin suddenly shouted, running over to a small stone area behind the building. The boys hustled over to where she was pointing.

Sam stopped short. "That's it?" He saw a life-size, dark bronze statue of President Lincoln sitting on a bench next to a young boy. "That is *not* what I was expecting."

"It's so small," said Derek.

Sam read the inscription on the stones in the wall behind the bench. "*TO BIND UP THE NATION'S WOUNDS*. How can a nation have wounds?"

"He must have brought a huge box of Band-Aids," said Derek.

"Probably because it was torn apart by the Civil War," said Caitlin.

"Right," said Derek. "That was my second guess."

Mrs. Murphy walked out toward them. An older man was next to her, but with the bright sun shining in his face, Sam couldn't tell who it was.

"Hello there, kids!" the man called.

Sam immediately recognized the voice. "Professor Evanshade! What are you doing here?" They had met the professor in two of their previous adventures. He'd given them a reward for finding the lost coins in the creek behind their house, and when they tracked down an early copy of the Declaration of Independence in Williamsburg with Caitlin, the professor had helped authenticate it.

"Oh golly," laughed the professor. He was always saying *golly*. "I make stops at several of the museums around town to keep things in tip-top shape. I saw y'all running out the rear entrance a few moments ago and wanted to say hello. I guessed this might be where you were headed."

He nodded at Mrs. Murphy. "Your chaperone here tells me you're learning about the Civil War."

"We're trying to, but it's pretty confusing," admitted Sam.

"Well, you've come to the right place." The old man gestured to the statue of Lincoln and the boy. "What do you think of it?"

"It's pretty small," said Derek.

"Is the boy President Lincoln's son?" asked Caitlin.

"Yes it is, young lady," answered the professor. "Young Tad was with the president when he visited Richmond."

"Lincoln came to Richmond?" asked Sam.

"He certainly did. That's why the statue is here. It was actually only placed here in 2003, so it hasn't been with us very long. There was quite a controversy, to be honest. Have a seat, and I'll tell you about Lincoln's visit. It's quite interesting."

Sam and Caitlin sat down along the wall. Derek sat next to Lincoln on the bronze bench that was part of the statue, but the professor didn't seem to mind.

"After General Lee's troops left the city, the president traveled by boat up the James River. He'd been nearby and wanted to tour the city of Richmond and show some compassion to the people who had endured the war for so long. His boat couldn't make it all the way to the city due to the rapids on the James and a group of sunken ships in the river. So he and his twelve-year-old son, Tad, disembarked at a spot just outside the city, called Rocketts Landing, with just a small group of soldiers, and walked the rest of the way. He toured the wreckage, visited the Confederate white house, and talked to the people, including many slaves."

"Wow, people must have been surprised to see him there," said Sam.

"Yes they were," answered the professor. "And it was quite a historic visit they had with him, too. Lincoln would be president for only four more days."

"Four days?" exclaimed Sam. "Was there a new election? Another war?" That didn't make sense at all. How could he free the slaves if he wasn't president?

"Wasn't Lincoln the president over the whole country again after Lee surrendered?" asked Caitlin.

"Yes and no," said the professor. "You see, Lincoln had hoped to leave Richmond to witness the surrender of Lee's army. But when a surrender didn't occur right away, after a couple of days, he returned to Washington and went to the theater."

"He saw a movie?" asked Derek.

"Ha! No, there weren't movies back then like we have today, Derek. He went to see a play."

Sam's brain was whirling. He almost remembered

what Professor Evanshade was talking about, but couldn't quite say it in time.

"Wait! I know what happened," shouted Caitlin. "He was shot!"

"That's right," said Sam. "I knew that. By John Wayne, right?"

The professor and Mrs. Murphy laughed.

"Close," said Mrs. Murphy.

Professor Evanshade stood, resting his hand on Lincoln's shoulder. "Lincoln was shot on April 14, 1865, at Ford's Theater in Washington. He died the next morning. The assassin *was* a famous actor, but not John Wayne. John Wilkes Booth snuck into the president's private balcony at the theater. After firing the shot, Booth jumped from the balcony down to the stage. He broke his leg, but still managed to escape on horseback. He was part of a plot to assassinate several leaders of the government, including the secretary of state and the vice president, but Lincoln was the only one who died."

"Wow. Did they hold a massive manhunt and catch him?" asked Derek.

"Actually, that's exactly what happened," said the professor, nodding. "Booth was tracked down several days later by Union soldiers and killed in a farmhouse between Washington and Richmond."

"Gosh, that's really sad," said Sam.

"Sad?" said Derek. "He killed the president! I'm glad they shot him."

"No, not Booth," said Sam. "President Lincoln. He made it all the way through the war and then was killed before he could enjoy the victory."

"It was a dark day for our nation," agreed the Professor.

"Who was president then?" asked Caitlin. "Jefferson Davis?"

"No," said the professor. "Davis' days in office were over. Vice President Andrew Johnson became president for a few years. After that, the voters elected Ulysses S. Grant."

"Wow. He was the Union general who defeated Lee," said Caitlin.

"I guess there's no statue on Monument Avenue for him either," said Sam.

Professor Evanshade shook his head. "No, there's not, Sam. That would have been a little too hard to take for the Southerners of Richmond, I'm afraid."

"That's quite a story," Mrs. Murphy said. "Isn't it, kids?"

"A true story," said Caitlin.

"Those are usually the best kind," said Professor Evanshade, stepping away from the statue. "Well, I hope you kids enjoyed the museum. It's great to see you again. Something tells me we'll be crossing paths again in the future."

"I hope so," said Derek. "That usually means we made a discovery!"

Sam looked down the hill to the James River. He pictured President Lincoln marching through the town, shaking people's hands a hundred and fifty years ago, not knowing he only had a few more days to live.

His thoughts were interrupted by three white, box trucks screeching to a stop at the edge of the parking lot. The words on the side of the trucks said they were from a party rental company.

"You're having a party?" Derek asked the professor.

"Yes, we are. A gala, actually, which is a big party. It's tomorrow night, right here at Tredegar. We're celebrating the one hundred and fiftieth anniversary of Lincoln's visit to Richmond. I'd love for y'all to join us." He turned to Mrs. Murphy. "That is, if it's okay with your parents."

"A party! Cool!" exclaimed Derek.

Caitlin grabbed her mom's arm. "Can we, Mom? That sounds like so much fun!"

"*And* educational!" said Sam.

"That's very nice of you, Professor," said Mrs. Murphy. "It's okay with me, but we'll have to ask your parents about it, boys."

"Wonderful!" exclaimed Professor Evanshade. "Your parents are welcome as well, of course. Just let us know."

Mrs. Murphy turned to the boys. "Speaking of your

parents, we need to get back. They're coming home in the morning, aren't they?"

Sam looked up from the statue at the mention of his parents' return. "Oh my gosh, you're right! We need to get home and get the house ready for them."

"If Meghan hasn't already burned it down," said Derek, shaking his head.

"All right then, let's get going," said Mrs. Murphy.

"Thanks for inviting us, Professor!" called Caitlin.

"Yeah, thanks, Professor!" yelled Sam, as he hustled down the pathway toward the car.

"You're welcome! I hope to see you tomorrow."

CHAPTER SIXTEEN

W hen the boys got back home, their house was still standing, but there was no sign of Meghan. The front door was locked and the minivan wasn't in the driveway.

"Where'd she go?" asked Derek, hands on his hips, squinting in the late afternoon sun.

"I'll give you one guess," answered Sam.

"Paul."

"Yep." He sat down next to Derek on the porch steps. Tomorrow couldn't come soon enough, in Sam's mind. Not only would Mom and Dad be home, but Meghan was leaving too. Or maybe she'd already left. That would be okay with him.

"You boys staging a protest?" Mr. Haskins called over the fence before Sam could dream further about life without Meghan.

"We're locked out," answered Derek.

"Where's that girl who was watching you? Did you drive her off?"

"We don't know," said Derek, shrugging his shoulders. "She's supposed to be here."

"Mom and Dad are coming home in the morning, though," added Sam. He liked saying that. Maybe if he kept saying it they'd get back sooner.

As they were speaking, a familiar green and white taxi pulled to the curb next to their mailbox. "Maybe that's your mystery girl now," cackled Mr. Haskins, pointing to the street.

Sam hopped up from the porch. "Is that Meghan?"

"Oh my gosh, I bet she crashed the minivan," cried Derek. "Mom and Dad are going to kill her."

A door opened and someone stepped out of the taxi into the sunlight. And then another person followed. Sam's heart leaped.

"Mom! Dad!" cried Derek, bolting across the yard.

Sam couldn't believe it. It *was* his parents—a day early! He raced over and joined Derek in giving Mom and Dad long hugs.

"Hey guys!" laughed his dad. "Surprise!"

"Hi honey," said his mom with a wide smile. She squeezed Sam tight.

"What are you doing here?" asked Sam. "I thought

you weren't supposed to be home until two in the morning?

Dad grinned. "Well, we had a slight change of plans," he explained. "Air traffic control in Paris was about to go on strike, so we switched to a direct flight and headed out a few hours early."

"Are you disappointed?" asked Mom. "Should we go back?"

"No!" the boys shouted in unison.

"Please stay," said Derek.

Sam closed his eyes and opened them again just to make sure he wasn't imagining things. He was so happy to see them. He'd missed them even more than he'd realized.

"Welcome home, folks," called Mr. Haskins, watching the family reunion from across the fence.

Dad waved back. "Thanks, Jonas. I hope these two didn't cause any trouble for you while we were gone."

"Hmph," cackled Mr. Haskins. "No more than usual, I guess." Sam thought he saw a faint smile on the old man's lips.

"Where's Meghan?" asked Mom, glancing around the yard.

"Well ..." said Sam.

"Maybe you should come inside and sit down first, Mom," suggested Derek. He picked up a bag and headed toward the house.

"Boys …" their dad said, nervously.

* * *

IT WAS dark when headlights flashed through Sam's bedroom window and a vehicle pulled into the driveway. He looked through the blinds to see Mom and Dad walk quickly off the front porch to the driveway.

"Uncle Bill, Aunt Ali … you're home!" Sam heard Meghan exclaim. She sounded nervous.

"Where have you been?" Mom answered, her voice filled with a mix of concern and frustration.

Sam had been worried about Meghan, too. She'd been mean the whole week, and she had given them a lot more freedom than their parents would have allowed, but she hadn't just abandoned them before. He watched Mom and Dad walk Meghan around to the backyard out of earshot, and sat back down on his bed.

Sam felt better with Mom and Dad back home. Things would be back to normal. He'd had enough of Meghan with her bad attitude and endless phone calls. He wondered what he'd be like when he was college-age. He hoped he wouldn't be as concerned about a girlfriend as Meghan was about Paul. Not that he could imagine having a girlfriend in the first place. Mom said he'd feel differently about girls when he got older, but he seriously doubted it.

"She's so busted," said Derek, standing in the doorway to Sam's room. He was holding an Eiffel Tower snow globe. Mom and Dad had also bought him a cool soccer jersey as promised.

Mom and Dad had tried to pretend like they'd forgotten Sam's present at the airport, but Dad couldn't keep a straight face. He eventually pulled a picture out of his suitcase of a two-foot replica of an Egyptian Sphinx. They'd bought the replica itself at the gift shop at the Louvre museum, but it was too big to put in their suitcase on the plane, so it was being shipped. Sam didn't know what to say, but it was pretty sweet! It would look great in his room—as long as Derek didn't break it.

* * *

WHEN SAM CAME DOWNSTAIRS for breakfast the next morning, Meghan was quietly carrying her bags down the hallway. Dad picked them up from by the front door and lugged them out to the van so he could drive her over to Paul's apartment. From there, Meghan and Paul were going to make the long drive up to New York.

"Bye," said Derek, standing at the door as Meghan stepped off the porch. Sam walked up to see her give a weak wave. She had a glum look on her face.

"Is she really leaving just like that?" asked Sam.

"I guess," said Derek. "Mom told me she got the

minivan stuck in a mud patch after seeing Paul yesterday up at the lake. She had to get a tow truck to pull it out. That's why she was so late."

"Why didn't she call?" Sam figured she could have at least done that.

"Her phone died and Paul had already left."

"Oh. That stinks," said Sam. He supposed that was a fairly good excuse, although he couldn't help thinking that if she'd spent more time with them instead of Paul, it might not have happened.

The boys watched the minivan pull down the driveway. Then it stopped. Meghan opened the door and ran back to the house.

"Did she forget something?" asked Derek.

Sam looked around the foyer. He didn't see anything. "What's the matter?" asked Sam, stepping out with Derek on the porch.

Meghan reached out with two arms and smothered them both in a long hug. "I'm sorry," she whispered. "I got my priorities mixed up."

Sam just nodded, not knowing what to say. He saw a tear slip down her cheek as she pulled back.

"Good luck with your cooking," said Derek, grinning.

Meghan wiped her face and forced a laugh. "You guys are okay." She turned and walked toward the van. "Take care of yourselves," she called over her shoulder with a wave.

CHAPTER SEVENTEEN

The sun was setting as the boys and their parents pulled into the parking lot at Tredegar. Things looked very different than they had just the day before. A huge white tent covered part of the courtyard in front of the museum. Two spotlights were set next to the cannons, piercing the sky with white tunnels of light that reminded Sam of Batman's bat signal.

"Wow!" exclaimed Derek. "It's like the Superbowl!"

Dad laughed. "A little smaller than that, but not bad, I'll admit."

"Nicer than Paris, Mom?" asked Sam.

"Hmm," she answered. "I don't think it can quite match the lights of Paris, but it's nice to be home."

The boys decided not to share all of what they'd been up to, but they had told their parents about Professor Evanshade's invitation to the gala. Although still weary from their trip, Mom and Dad could see the boys' excitement, so they'd agreed to come. Sam promised Derek he wouldn't bring up anything about the Confederate Ghosts. There was no reason to get Mom and Dad worked up about it. Sam was sure they'd seen the last of the bikers anyhow.

The crowd at the gala buzzed with groups of people under the tent and at tables on both sides of the courtyard. Waiters in black suits carrying trays of tall champagne glasses filtered through the crowd, and musicians with violins and a big cello played classical music near the cannons.

Despite being next to the river, it was muggy in the summer night. Sam tugged at his shirt collar, feeling out of place at such a fancy event. Mom had made them wear collared shirts and brown khaki pants. He felt like he was at church on Easter. At least Derek had talked her out of making them wear ties.

"Sam!" a familiar voice called. Caitlin was walking toward them across the courtyard wearing a flowery dress.

"Hey there," he answered.

"Hi!" She reached out and gave him a hug, sending Derek into a snicker. Sam wished she didn't have to act so friendly. It was embarrassing and only fueled Derek's teasing.

"Hi, Derek. Isn't this just amazing?" Caitlin spread

her arm like a game show host toward the courtyard. "You have to try the punch. It's *so* good."

"Hello, Caitlin," said Mom. "It's good to see you. How's your summer going?"

"Hi, Mr. and Mrs. Jackson. Welcome back! I'm so glad you could come. How was Paris?"

Mom let a yawn slip out. "It was wonderful, but we're still trying to get used to the time change, honestly." She draped her arm through Dad's, looking up at him sleepily.

"But this isn't such a bad thing to come home to," Dad added. "Where are your parents hiding, Caitlin?"

"Down there by the food." She pointed to a long table covered by a white cloth. "Mom says the tuna tartar is to die for. It sounds gross to me."

Even from a distance, Sam could see a man in a chef's hat standing over a big hunk of meat at the far end of the table. Sam's mouth was already watering as the smells wafted up to where they were standing.

"We're going to go walk around, okay, Dad?" said Derek.

"After we get some food," corrected Sam.

"Okay, but stay nearby," said Dad.

"And behave yourselves," said Mom. "This is a very nice event. I don't want to see you running around and causing trouble."

"Okay, we will," echoed the boys, turning toward the food table.

"Oh, and be sure to find Professor Evanshade and thank him for inviting us," she called after them.

Derek gave her a thumbs up as they hurried off.

Caitlin laughed at the expressions on the boys' faces. "No more free rein, I guess, with your parents home." She tugged Sam's arm toward the courtyard. "Come on, I want you to try this punch!"

* * *

THE RIVER WAS DARK, but reflections from the spotlights danced across the water in a hazy glow. Sam's plate was filled to overflowing as he sat on a bench facing the river.

"Are you going to eat all of those?" asked Caitlin.

As if on cue, Sam picked up a shrimp, dipped it in a glob of tartar sauce on the side of his plate, and took a big bite. "Yes," he mumbled through a mouthful. "This food is so good. I could eat here for a year."

Derek walked down to the water's edge and picked up a stone. "How far do you think I can throw it?"

Before Sam could answer, Caitlin set her plate down on the bench and stood up with a rock in her hand too. "Not as far as me!"

"What?" said Derek. "No way."

"Why, because I'm a girl?"

"Well—" Derek paused, trying to think of a good explanation. "Yeah, that's exactly why."

"Don't bet on it," said Caitlin.

Sam remembered Caitlin surprising him with her back dive at the pool. He wouldn't put anything past her, although he didn't think she could out-throw Derek.

"Okay … watch this. I bet that I can make it half way to Belle Isle." Derek stepped back, dramatically stretching his arm like he was getting all limbered up.

"Oh, brother," moaned Sam. "Get on with it already."

Derek wound up, took two quick steps, and hurled the stone far out into the river. He stood, holding his arm extended in his follow through, as if anticipating a roar from the crowd.

"Where'd it go?" asked Sam. "I didn't hear a splash. Maybe you missed the river."

"It's too dark. We can't see it," said Caitlin.

"It must have hit Belle Isle," said Derek. "That means I'm the automatic winner!"

"You couldn't hit the island," said Sam. "Nobody could throw it *that* far."

A shower of pebbles came from out of nowhere, raining down on them and the bench.

"Ouch!" shrieked Caitlin.

"What the—," said Derek, turning around to see what was happening. "Oh no …" His expression sank.

"Hey Jackson, whatcha doing over here in the dark?" a familiar voice called.

It was Cameron and his sidekick, Sean.

"Oh, and look, it's Sammy and his little lady. Do your mommies know you're over here?"

Caitlin turned and stepped back toward the gala. "Come on, let's go."

"Not so fast, girlie," Cameron yelled, grabbing Caitlin by the wrist and pushing her down onto the park bench.

"Ow, stop it! That hurts, you jerk!" She tried to elbow him in the stomach, but he was too strong and pushed her back down by the shoulders.

"Just sit tight for a second. We want to talk to your friend here," said Cameron, looking at Derek.

Derek walked right up to the bully's face. "Knock it off, Cameron. What do you want?"

Sam stood next to his brother. "Let go of her," he yelled.

"Oh, did we make you mad, Little Jackson?" Cameron cackled, raising his hands in the air. "Fine, stay with your girlfriend. It's your brother that we want to talk to anyway."

Caitlin jumped up and moved behind Sam and Derek. "Let's go back. Our parents are waiting for us right over there."

"Oh, I don't think they can hear you from here," said Sean with a grin. "Not with all that music playing and the people talking."

"What are you even doing here, Cameron?" asked Derek, nodding toward the big tent and the lights. "I didn't know you cared about history."

"I don't," said Cameron, laughing. "But my parents are big donors to the museum, so they made me come along. I thought it would be lame, but things just got a lot more fun!" He put his arm around Derek's shoulder. "We have this little problem that we need your help with, Jackson."

Sean let out another of his hyena laughs, nodding his head. "Yeah, we need your help."

"My bud, Sean, here, left his favorite hat over by the hydro plant on the island yesterday, and he really wants it back." Cameron pointed across the water to Belle Isle's dark outline.

"That's a real shame," said Derek, "but I'm sure you can find it."

"The thing is, Sean's kind of tired today, so he doesn't feel like going all the way across the bridge to get it."

Sean hung his head. "I don't think I got enough sleep last night."

"That's where you come in, Jackson," said Cameron, glancing at Sam and Caitlin to make sure they were paying attention. "All you have to do is walk across the bridge, go over to the hydro plant, fetch his hat, and bring it back to us. After that, we'll leave you alone for the whole year at school. Wouldn't that be nice?"

"Gee, thanks," said Derek, "but I think I'll take my chances at school. Good luck with your hat." He started walking past the teenagers toward the party. "Come on, guys."

Sam and Caitlin turned to follow him, but Cameron and Sean stepped in front, grabbing them both by the wrists.

"Hey, cut it out!" yelled Sam, as Cameron's hands squeezed his forearm tightly. He tried to wriggle loose, but Cameron was too strong.

"I don't think you're hearing me, Jackson. Do it, or else your brother and his girlfriend are going to go for a little swim in the river." His face broke into an evil grin. "I hear it's really hard to see the rocks coming in the rapids in the dark. It would be a real shame if one of them banged their head."

Sam pulled again at Cameron's grasp but wasn't getting anywhere. He tried to think about what to do. Why had they left the party?

"All right, I'll do it," blurted Derek. "Just let them go, will you?"

Sam shook his head at his brother.

"I thought you'd see it my way," said Cameron, easing

his grip on Sam's arms and nodding to Sean to do the same with Caitlin.

"Don't do it, Derek. They're just trying to get you mad," said Caitlin.

Derek shook his head. "I have to stand up to them sometime. Besides, I just have to go over to the island and get Sean's stupid hat. We were just there the other day. I know the way. I'll come right back."

Derek stepped forward, toward the bridge. "Okay, let's get this over with." He pointed at Sam and Caitlin. "But leave them alone. Give me your word."

Sam knew Cameron's word wouldn't mean a whole lot since he was a big liar. He wished Derek wasn't doing this.

Cameron raised his hands up in the air again like he was innocent. "I swear. We won't touch them." He motioned toward the bridge. "Now get going."

Derek looked at Sam and Caitlin. "You guys stay here. I'll be right back."

"You don't even have a flashlight," said Caitlin. "It's really dark up there."

"I'll tell you what, Jackson," said Cameron. "Since I'm such a nice guy, I'll let you borrow my flashlight just this once so your little friend here doesn't cry, okay?" He pulled a thin flashlight out of his pocket and handed it to Derek.

Derek took the light, flicked its narrow beam on to

make sure it worked, and, without another word, sprinted out of sight toward the stairs to the bridge.

Sam turned and stared at Cameron and Sean. "What's the matter with you guys? Don't you have anything better to do than bother us?"

Cameron and Sean started cracking up even more than usual.

"What's so funny?" asked Caitlin.

Sean pulled a hat out of his back pocket. "He's going to have a hard time finding this over there!"

"Derek! Come back. It's a trick!" yelled Sam, turning back to the bridge, but he was too late. Derek's dim light was already bouncing along the concrete bridge as he ran toward Belle Isle, too far away to hear Sam's voice.

"You're such a jerk!" yelled Caitlin, socking Cameron in the stomach.

"Oomph," Cameron moaned at Caitlin's surprisingly strong punch. He stepped forward to retaliate when Sean interrupted him.

"Dude, look over there!" Sean pointed across the river to Belle Isle.

Everyone turned and looked across the water. "What is it?" asked Cameron.

"Right there," said Sean. "A light. That can't be Jackson. He couldn't be over there already, and it's too bright for his flashlight."

Sam stared harder at the island until a flash of light

caught his eye. Before he could focus on it, the light was gone. Was it coming from the island or just a reflection off the water? He thought of Mr. Haskins' ghosts battling over the rapids and gulped.

He counted two beats before he saw it again, moving across the island. Was it a flashlight? It would have to be a pretty strong beam to shine that brightly. Sean was right—Derek was a fast runner, but there was no way he could have gotten that far already. Maybe it was a reflection.

"There's another one!" shouted Caitlin. "And another. See them?"

Sam watched two more lights follow the first slowly through the trees. "They're moving—like headlights." He looked at Caitlin. "Motorcycle headlights!"

"The Confederate Ghosts!" she exclaimed.

"Ghosts?" laughed Cameron. "You two are way too gullible." He turned to Sean and motioned toward the party. "I don't know *what* that is, but it's Jackson's problem now. Come on, Sean, let's get out of here."

They walked up toward the gala. "Good luck, Sammy. Oh, and tell your chicken brother we found Sean's hat so the deal is off." They laughed as they raced off toward the party.

Sam had the sinking feeling in his stomach that he got whenever he was in trouble. He thought he might puke. He pictured Mad Dog Dewitt riding around the island in the dark. "They must be heading to their hideout by the hydro plant. See how the headlights are all moving in that direction?"

"Isn't the island closed at night?" asked Caitlin. "How would they even get over there?"

"I think there's an access road on the other end. You're not supposed to, but I'll bet they drove over from that side."

"I wonder if Derek will see them from the bridge," said Caitlin.

Sam watched the lights move across the darkness. He remembered the ceremony at Jefferson Davis' grave—the blood ceremony. "Let's get back to the party and tell my Mom and Dad."

"What? No, we have to go after him," said Caitlin.

Sam looked at her to see if she was kidding. She must be. That was a *terrible* idea. "Are you crazy? I hated that bridge in the daylight. I'm not going over it at night."

"What if something happens to him, Sam? You can't just leave him there."

"That's why we need to get my parents. It's too dark to go ourselves, and we don't even have a flashlight."

Caitlin held up her hand. "Hang on, wait right here." She ran toward the gala before he could object.

Sam stood alone, wondering what to do. He couldn't see Derek's light on the bridge anymore. It was like he'd been sucked up by the darkness of the island. The ghost island. Why were they even considering going after him alone? He imagined what the Ghosts could be doing out there. As he pictured the worst in his mind, he saw Caitlin running back toward him.

"Ta-da," she announced, pulling a flashlight from behind her back.

"Where did you get that?"

"I saw it sitting on the waiters' stand by the food table before we walked out here. I grabbed it when no one was looking."

"You stole it?"

"No, just borrowed," said Caitlin. "This is an emergency. I'll give it back when we're done."

She started walking toward the stairs to the bridge, following the way Derek had gone. "Come on. Let's go."

Sam hesitated for a moment then groaned loudly. "Hold up," he called, jogging behind her. "Wait for me."

CHAPTER EIGHTEEN

As they moved closer to the bridge, the concrete path wound upward, like the hallway ramps in a baseball stadium. After the last corner, they came to a metal gate with bars running top to bottom, like in a prison cell. A chain was wrapped around the gate and held together with a padlock.

"It's locked," said Sam, tugging on the bars. The doors pulled a few inches toward him until they were caught by the chain. "How did Derek get across? It's too high to climb."

He stared over the side of the bridge, listening to the water speed through the rapids below. He wondered if Cameron would have really tried to throw them in the river. He was probably just bluffing, but Sam was glad he didn't have to find out for sure.

"Like this," said Caitlin.

Sam turned back to the gate only to see Caitlin standing on the other side. She held the chain over her head with her hand. "It's loose enough to squeeze through. Come on!"

"Oh … I knew that," Sam said, sheepishly. "But I think they have the chain there for a reason, you know."

"Just come on, Sam. We have to help Derek."

Sam hoped he hadn't eaten too many shrimp earlier as he sucked in his stomach, squeezing between the metal bars. "I'm going to send a complaint letter to the mayor about this gate," he muttered.

"Come on," Caitlin called, already running ahead.

The walking bridge was creepy. Despite Caitlin's flashlight, it was still dark. It was like a mini-bridge, hanging from huge cables beneath the highway bridge, which loomed above them like a roof without walls.

Sam reminded himself that the bridge was made of concrete, so it should be sturdy enough. But at the same time, concrete was very heavy, so it might be too much for the cables to hold. He shuddered at the thought of the cables snapping, and falling to his doom into the river below.

It was probably his imagination, but it seemed like the bridge was swaying. The flow of the river below and the echoes of the traffic above created an eerie symphony that faded in and out with the breeze.

Finally, they reached the end of the bridge, zigzagging

through another ramp and onto Belle Isle. They stood perfectly still for a few moments, listening to the sounds of the island. The roar of the traffic on the bridge was farther away now, but the river's noise was still all around. The only light to be seen was from their flashlight, which suddenly went dark.

"Hey!" shouted Sam.

"Sorry," said Caitlin, flicking it back on. "My finger slipped on the switch." She giggled. "Did you think the ghosts had gotten us?"

"No," said Sam, although he may have thought that for a second. He looked around him in the darkness. "Where did Derek go?"

"He was heading for the hydro plant. So, which way is that?"

Sam tried to remember from their bike ride the other day, but he felt turned around in the dark. "I think it's this way," he said, hesitantly. "Let's go toward those trees to see if we can spot the trail." They jogged to the tree line until Caitlin grabbed his arm.

"Look, over there!" she whispered.

Sam turned and saw a light moving between the trees and then it disappeared. Was it Derek? A motorcycle headlight? Or something else? It didn't matter. They had to keep going now. "Come on, he's got to be this way."

The flashlight beam landed on the old brick wall Sam had explored with Derek. Sam led Caitlin through the rugged archway to the hidden trail behind, walking softly to keep their arrival secret.

"We have to be close to the hydro plant now," Sam whispered. "Stay quiet."

They crept forward, spying the dark shadows of the hydro plant building against the night sky. A dim light glowed through the trees. It looked like a fire. Were the woods burning? They had to get closer.

Voices echoed through the walls of the hydro plant building. Sam felt nervous again as they crept up to one of the windows. What was he even doing there? He should have told Mom and Dad, they would have known what to do. Now he and Caitlin were in danger too, with no idea where Derek was.

"Look," whispered Caitlin, peering through the metal bars in the window. Three burly men in leather vests were huddled around a campfire, talking quietly.

Bikers. The Confederate Ghosts!

The ghost mural seemed to dance through the dim shadows from the flames. When one of the men bent down to poke the logs in the campfire with a stick, Sam muffled a groan.

Sitting in the corner of the room was Derek. He'd been captured by the Ghosts! Sam hadn't seen him until the big man moved.

Caitlin's eyes opened wide as she saw Derek too. Her mouth opened but made no sound. Were they holding him hostage? From their distance, Sam couldn't tell if Derek was hurt, but knew he must be scared.

It wasn't hard to imagine what must have happened. Derek had run into the hydro plant to retrieve Sean's stupid hat. The bikers must have already been there, or had run into him along the way. Then they had grabbed him. What could they possibly want with a kid like Derek? Sam gulped, remembering the blood ceremony by Jefferson Davis' grave, and how he had predicted the Ghosts would be looking for Northern kids to sacrifice.

"We have to do something," he whispered into Caitlin's ear. They couldn't just stand there and let Derek die.

"I know, but what?" Caitlin whispered back.

Sam stared at his big brother beyond the fire, then up at the haunting ghost mural. He remembered how they'd been in tight spots before—they'd run from a bear near the mines in the woods, even outsmarted a bad guy in a dark colonial garden. Somehow, those things had worked out okay, so what should they do now? Then it came to him. They needed a distraction! But what?

"Follow me," he whispered to Caitlin, crouching low under the window and stepping around the outside of the building. Together, they turned the corner and went down a slope to where the basement level of the hydro plant backed up to the edge of the river. He stopped short as three large, low shadows came into view.

"What is *that*?" whispered Caitlin.

Sam froze, studying the shadows, worried they might be more men. The shadows weren't moving, and they were too big to be rocks. Then he realized what they were —motorcycles! Three big Harleys were parked along the lower level of the building a few yards from the river. He remembered hearing the voices the first time he and Derek had explored the hydro plant. This must be the lower entrance where the bikers had arrived.

In a flash, he knew what the distraction would be. "What do bikers care about more than anything?" he whispered to Caitlin.

"What?"

"Their bikes! It's a perfect distraction." They'd just have to be quick.

Caitlin smiled and nodded in agreement.

Sam crept closer, pushing lightly on the nearest bike to gauge its weight. It was heavy, but he figured if they both pushed on it at once, it would topple into the other two and they would fall like dominoes.

Moving back up the slope, Sam stopped under a window that was closer to the campfire and Derek. The bikers were looking away, so Sam decided to take a chance. He stood up in front of the window, waving to get Derek's attention. Maybe it was the darkness, or the glare from the fire, but Derek didn't see him, and the men were too close for Sam to call out.

Sam crouched back down under the window next to Caitlin. "I can't just keep waving. One of them is going to turn around and see me. We have to let him know we're here so he can be ready to run."

"What about this?" Caitlin held up a small pebble, motioning it toward the window. Sam nodded his head. It could work.

He reached out his hand to take the pebble, but Caitlin was already standing at the window, her arm cocked to throw. Sam grimaced as she tossed the pebble, fearing that it might hit one of the metal bars, but it sailed right through.

Derek's arm jerked like something had bitten him.

Bullseye!

Sam and Caitlin both jumped into the center of the window, silently waving their arms back and forth. Derek raised his head, his eyes flashing surprise, before glancing back at the bikers and resuming a normal expression. He peeked back up at them casually. Sam held up one finger to indicate that he should wait for them. Derek gave a slight nod to show he understood.

Sam and Caitlin ducked below the window and hustled back down the slope to the bikes. "Ready?" Sam whispered.

Caitlin nodded as they placed their hands on the first motorcycle, Sam's on the seat and Caitlin's next to the handlebars. As quietly as he could, Sam counted out,

"One, two, three!" They heaved their weight into the bike with all their might.

The bike toppled to its side, clanging into the next bike, which crashed into the third. All three toppled to the ground, the clanging of metal piercing the silence.

"Boom!" Sam shouted, adding to the noise.

Sam and Caitlin immediately raced past the pile of motorcycles and up the slope on the other side of the building. Sam prayed that Derek had gotten the message and was making a run for it.

As they ran, Sam heard the men shouting in the building. "The bikes!" yelled one of them, his head at the window. Sam made it to the trail just in time to see Derek leaping from the metal bars, landing hard on the ground, but staying on his feet.

"Derek, over here!" called Caitlin, softly.

"What are you guys doing?" Derek said, pausing in front of them.

"We're rescuing you!" said Sam. "It looked like you could use some help."

Derek smiled. "Thanks! But we have to get out of here!"

They turned toward the trail, but before they could take another step, a bright light flicked on just ahead of them. They all froze, shielding their eyes from the blinding light with their arms.

"That's far enough," a deep voice growled from behind the light.

Sam's blood ran cold. He had thought they were home free. Caitlin reached over and squeezed his hand. They heard the sound of footsteps walking toward them as a tall silhouette came into the light. They stood, paralyzed, as the figure walked closer. Sam heard the other men running up behind them. There was nowhere to go.

They were trapped.

The man moved closer until they could see his face through the light.

Sam gasped.

It was Mad Dog DeWitt.

CHAPTER NINETEEN

"Don't move." Mad Dog glared down at them through the bright light. Sam realized it had to be the headlight from his motorcycle, just like the other lights they'd seen moving through the woods from across the river.

Mad Dog looked past them to the other men. "What's going on here?" His voice was deep and gruff, as though he'd smoked too many cigarettes or gargled with gravel all his life. His beard was thick and black, mixed with flecks of gray. Sam looked up at his eyes and realized that DeWitt was older than he'd expected. Maybe that meant he'd killed more than just one man in a card game.

"The one kid came into the hideout just as we rolled in," said one of the other men. "He claimed to be looking for a hat or something, but we didn't believe him."

"Jonny thinks he might be a spy from Hopewell," added another man.

Sam's heart sank, imagining how a Union spy sneaking into Confederate territory might be captured and tortured. He wondered which of his fingers they would break first. He was too young to die!

Mad Dog groaned, glancing down at the kids. "Sit down," he ordered, pointing to a fallen log on the ground. They all did as they were told.

"We're sorry we got in your way," said Derek. "We didn't see anything."

"Our parents are at the gala over at Tredegar," added Caitlin. "They'll be looking for us any minute."

Sam glanced around nervously, knowing the gala was too far away for anyone to hear their screams. He thought of Mom and Dad. He might never see them again, and he'd barely even gotten to talk with them since they had returned from their trip.

"We won't tell anyone about your hideout. We promise," said Sam. "Just let us go."

"Quiet!" said Mad Dog, turning toward his partners. "What did you tell these kids? Do they think you're kidnapping them? That's just what we need ..." He glanced back at them on the log. "You boneheads actually think these kids are spies? Since when do they send little girls in flowery dresses as spies?"

The men were silent, searching for an answer. "Uh,

that's why they're spies," one of them finally stammered. "They're in *disguise*."

Mad Dog shook his head wearily, stepping over to his bike. He flicked off the headlight, sending everyone into sudden darkness until Caitlin turned on her flashlight.

Mad Dog turned toward them, crouching on his heels so he could look in their eyes. "What are your names?"

"Derek."

"Caitlin."

"Uh, Sam, Mr. Mad Dog, sir," Sam said, before he realized what he was saying. Derek nudged him with his elbow. "I mean, Mr. DeWitt, sir."

The big man was silent for a moment. Sam held his breath, wondering if this was how it felt to know you were going to die.

But then the strangest thing happened.

Mad Dog burst out laughing. It was a loud, deep-bellied laugh. "So, you know who I am, do you, kid? Very interesting. Maybe I'm more notorious than I thought. How old are you kids?"

Derek answered quickly before Sam could say anything else. "I'm twelve and these two are ten."

DeWitt stood up. Gosh, thought Sam, he's as tall as a tree.

"Listen, kids, no one is going to hurt you," Mad Dog said, looking at the others. "Isn't that right, boys?"

"Oh, sure."

"Absolutely. We're not savages."

"My name's Luke," said Mad Dog. "And this is Jonny, that's Chris, and over there's Bobby Ray."

Caitlin turned her head. "Wait a minute, but aren't you the Confederate Ghosts? We heard you were a dangerous biker gang."

"Yeah, that's us. But I'm afraid we've gotten a bad rap over the years," said Mad Dog. "We're just a bunch of guys who love riding our bikes and celebrating our Southern pride." He turned to the others. "Isn't that right, boys?"

"You know it, Luke!"

"God bless the South!"

Sam's mind was whirling. What kind of biker gang was this? "But we saw you on Monument Avenue circling the Robert E. Lee statue. You almost ran me over outside the bookstore!"

"That was you?" Mad Dog laughed. "Well, what were you doing stepping into the road in front of traffic? You look smarter than that. As for our parade, we were commemorating the General and the courage of our brothers who fought in the War of Northern Aggression. There's nothing wrong with that."

"Northern Aggression?" asked Caitlin. "Don't you mean the Civil War?"

Mad Dog grunted and looked over at his buddies.

"Well, that's a matter of perspective, missy. We can agree to disagree on that point tonight."

"Wasn't nothing *civil* about that war, no sir," said the biker named Chris.

"And what about Hollywood Cemetery?" asked Derek. "We saw you by the Jefferson Davis statue."

Bobby Ray stepped toward them, pointing. "See! They're following us, Luke! I told you they were Hopewell spies. I think we should hold them."

"Shut up, Chris," ordered Mad Dog. "I think you three have done enough to scare these kids tonight." He looked down at Derek. "You weren't supposed to see that, son. It was a private moment for our club, something that's been celebrated for years. There's nothing all that terrible about it. We were just paying our annual respects to our Confederate president. Jeff Davis was a good man. We have celebrations for other presidents, don't we?"

"Yeah," answered Derek.

"Well, no difference," said Mad Dog.

Sam tried to process all this new information. "So you aren't going to use us as a Northern blood sacrifice?"

Derek covered his face with his hand, and Caitlin gave a nervous giggle. Even as he said it, Sam realized how crazy that sounded.

All four men burst out laughing.

"Hey, Jonny, is this the week for the blood sacrifices, or is it next week?" Mad Dog hollered.

"No, I think it was last week," said Jonny. "But maybe we should hold them for some extra inventory." He laughed some more. "If I'd known the kid was a Yankee, I'd have held him a little tighter!"

Sam felt his cheeks turning red in the darkness. He decided to keep his mouth shut from now on.

Mad Dog turned back to them. "So what are you kids really doing out here on the island at night?"

"Yeah, if you're not spies," said the biker named Chris.

"Well, it's kind of my fault," said Derek. "A couple of jerks from my school forced me to come across the bridge to get one of their hats."

"But there really wasn't a hat," said Caitlin.

"Sean had it in his pocket the whole time," said Sam.

Derek turned to Sam in surprise. "He did?" He looked down at the ground. "I'm such an idiot. I should have just ignored them."

Mad Dog spoke up. "Sounds like you have a bully in your midst, son." He turned to Billy Ray and Chris. "What do we do with bullies around here, boys?"

Billy Ray's eyes narrowed as he spoke in a deep voice. "We gut 'em and feed 'em to the river ghosts." He let out a sinister laugh.

River ghosts? Sam didn't want to think about that again.

Derek leaned over to Mad Dog. "I thought *you* were the ghosts, no?"

"Yeah, isn't that why you have that painting on the wall back there?" said Sam, pointing back to the hydro plant.

"There's no such thing as ghosts for real," said Caitlin.

"Don't think so, huh?" chuckled Mad Dog. He leaned up against a tree, glancing through the darkness. "Do y'all know what this island used to be back in the war?"

"A prisoner-of-war camp," answered Sam.

Mad Dog nodded. "Correct, but a lot of Yankees never made it off of this island. They're still here, buried in the ground."

"We've heard this story," said Derek. "About how the Union ghosts fight with the Confederate soldier ghosts on the river."

"It's just a story," said Caitlin.

"Maybe, maybe not," said Mad Dog. "But let me tell ya, I've seen some things that make a man wonder." He looked off in the direction of the rapids.

"What kind of things?" asked Derek.

"Lights. When there's no moon. No vehicles. No flashlights. Dancing over the river. Strange sounds near the rapids."

Sam shivered. He didn't want to hear any more ghost

stories, especially out here in the dark with a biker gang. He stood up from the log. "I think we need to get going."

Mad Dog chuckled. "Yeah, I guess it's getting late. If your parents are really over at Tredegar, we need to get you back before they start missing you."

Derek looked over at the motorcycle behind Mad Dog and grinned. "Got any extra helmets?"

CHAPTER TWENTY

"I don't think this is a good idea ..." said Sam as he climbed up onto the seat behind Mad Dog. He'd thought Derek was joking when he suggested the bikers give them a ride back to the gala on their motorcycles. For some reason, DeWitt thought it was funny and agreed. He seemed strangely nice, in a gruff sort of way, considering he was supposed to be such a bad dude. Sam tried to remind himself that the other three guys had held Derek in the hydro plant, but they seemed more dumb than mean. Mad Dog was definitely the leader for a reason.

While Sam sat on the back of Mad Dog's bike, Derek climbed onto Jonny's and Caitlin onto Chris' bike. Billy Ray, the fourth member of the gang, hung back to keep an eye out for any other Ghost members who might show up. Mad Dog seemed to be most annoyed at Billy Ray, since it had been his idea to hold Derek.

Mad Dog's extra helmet was too big on Sam's head, so they tightened the chinstrap until it almost choked him. He still didn't feel very safe, but Mad Dog told him to hold onto his chest tightly, and said that they wouldn't go too fast. Anything more than standing still was too fast for Sam, but he kept his mouth shut.

Mad Dog bounced his weight on the motorcycle, kicking a pedal near the ground as the beast roared to life. For a moment, Sam worried that Mad Dog was going to tear off into the woods like a rocket, but instead, he eased forward slowly, making a gradual turn onto the trail.

Sam tried to be calm. Everything had gotten crazy since they'd run into Cameron and Sean by the water. He gave a nervous wave back to Caitlin. She didn't seem overly worried about the ride. Derek looked like he was having the time of his life, ready to do enormous motocross jumps over mounds of dirt like they'd seen on TV, if given the chance.

The brothers looked a bit ridiculous wearing their collared shirts and khaki pants with the big helmets. Caitlin in her flowered dress and Chris's spare helmet was something Sam had never thought he would see. They were quite a contrast to Mad Dog and his crew, all in black leather vests with their tattoo-covered arms.

"My grandson is about your age." Mad Dog's voice

rang through Sam's head. The helmets must have microphones in them. Did he say grandson? How could Mad Dog DeWitt be old enough to have a grandson? He was supposed to be young and mean and wild.

"Is he in the gang, too?" asked Sam.

Mad Dog chuckled. "Nah, he's in school just like you. Everything isn't always as sinister as it might appear to be, Sam."

"So I guess you're going to tell me that you didn't kill a man over a game of cards either?" Sam figured he might as well ask, since his life was now in this guy's hands. He was starting to feel a bit more relaxed on the bike as they rode along the trail.

"Killed a man, huh? Is that what you heard?" Mad Dog's voice came back through the helmet with a distorted mechanical tin to it. There was silence for a while. "No, I never killed anyone, kid. Although, I did do a lot of dumb things when I was younger. I paid for it too. Spent three years in the state pen over at Wallens Ridge."

Sam was pretty sure that meant prison. He thought about Mr. Haskins' story. "Were you playing cards?"

Mad Dog chuckled again. "Well, there may have been a game of cards involved, but no murders. I can promise you that."

"Are we going over the suspension bridge?" Sam asked.

"Nah, that bridge isn't for vehicles. We're going out the back of the island and over the Lee Bridge. You have a helmet on, so we're legal. Hang tight!"

Sam tightened his grip around Mad Dog's vest. He looked back and saw two headlights following close behind, but he couldn't see anyone's faces in the darkness. He hoped Caitlin was doing all right, and that Derek wasn't trying to drive.

The bike slowed, turning around a metal fence, then went down a long narrow straightaway next to the train tracks. They sped up as the tires hit the blacktop of the main road, and soon they were flying along on the highway that ran above the suspension bridge and across the river.

The giant spotlights from the gala at Tredegar lit up the sky as Mad Dog turned along the water. Sam wondered if Mom and Dad or Caitlin's parents had noticed they were missing. His stomach turned when he thought about explaining where they'd gone, but he was glad to be safe—as safe as he could be riding on the back of a motorcycle in the dark with a biker named Mad Dog.

Two figures were walking along the side of the road as they approached the parking lot. It was Cameron and Sean. "Stop!" Sam called into the helmet microphone, squeezing Mad Dog's chest tighter.

"What's the matter?"

"Up there." Sam pointed up the road. "It's the kids who made Derek run onto the island."

Mad Dog put his foot down on the pavement to steady the bike. "Really ... well maybe we should teach them a little lesson. What do you think?"

"That would be sweet!" said Sam, smiling inside his helmet.

Mad Dog motioned at the other two bikes to follow his lead. Sam slid off the seat and Derek and Caitlin quickly joined him on the pavement behind the motorcycles. Cameron and Sean had stopped walking and were staring at the three headlights that were moving in their direction. Sam remembered how it felt to stand in front of Mad Dog's headlight. He hoped the teenagers were as worried as he had been.

"What's going on?" asked Caitlin, as they followed behind the bikes.

"I don't know exactly," said Sam, "but just watch. I think this is going to be good."

Derek moved over next to them. "Who is that up there?"

"Who do you think?" replied Sam, grinning wide.

"Oh, yeah," said Derek, now recognizing Cameron's face. "That's perfect!"

Mad Dog walked his motorcycle forward slowly, revving the engine in loud bursts. Cameron and Sean stood frozen on the side of the road, lit up like Christmas ornaments. They tried to turn in the other direction, but Chris and Jonny closed in the circle. Cameron and Sean were boxed in like a couple of sheep in a pen.

Derek walked closer, standing just behind the bikes, but still invisible because of the lights.

"Where are you two jokers going?" Mad Dog's voice boomed out over the idling motorcycles. "Shouldn't you ladies be home with your mommies?"

Cameron and Sean's faces had turned pale. Ghost white. They looked around frantically for an escape. Sam would have almost felt bad for them if it hadn't been for what they'd done earlier. He figured they deserved a good scare.

"Hey, we're just walking," Cameron said.

"Yeah, what do you want?" asked Sean. His hyena laugh had vanished now that the tables were turned.

"That's a nice hat, kid," barked Mad Dog.

Sean touched the hat on his head with a concerned *who me?* look on his face.

"Bring it to me," Mad Dog ordered.

Sean didn't move. Sam figured he must be about to pee his pants. Sam couldn't see Derek's face since he was up closer to the bikes, but he knew he must have been smiling. Sam nudged Caitlin and tried to hold in a laugh.

"Do it!" yelled Mad Dog.

Sean reluctantly tugged the hat from his head and shuffled forward to the unseen voice. He stretched his arm out into the light until Mad Dog snatched the hat from his hand. Sean scampered back to Cameron, shaking his head.

Mad Dog leaned his motorcycle onto its kickstand and passed the hat back to Derek. He placed his arm around Derek's shoulder, and they both stepped forward into the light.

Cameron's face sank when he saw Derek next to Mad Dog. "You've got to be kidding me …" he groaned.

"Jackson?" said Sean, still too surprised to realize what was happening.

"I see you two dimwits know my friend, Derek," said Mad Dog.

"Yeah …" Cameron muttered, looking down at his feet.

"What?" growled Mad Dog. "Look at me, kid."

"Yes, sir," Cameron said, bending his neck up to see Mad Dog's scruffy face.

"Derek here is one of my boys," said Mad Dog. "He's not to be touched at school, out of school, anywhere. Understood?"

"Yes, sir," Cameron and Sean said quickly.

"If I hear of any more trouble with Derek, his brother, or his friends, you two will answer to me." Mad Dog placed his hand on Cameron's shoulder, staring down into his eyes. "And kid, you're not gonna want to answer to me, are you?"

Cameron shook his head so fast Sam thought it might come unscrewed.

"Thanks for the hat, Sean," said Derek, turning and walking behind the bikes toward Sam and Caitlin.

Sam couldn't help it and let a chuckle sneak out. This was great!

"Now get out of here before I change my mind and feed you to the river ghosts!" hollered Mad Dog. He raised his foot and kicked Cameron in the rear. Sean and Cameron took off running like a ghost was already chasing them. Maybe in some ways, a ghost really was chasing them, but not the kind they thought.

A Confederate Ghost.

Mad Dog walked back to his motorcycle and gave a fist bump to Derek. "Good?"

Derek smiled excitedly. "Better than good. That was fantastic!"

Mad Dog laughed. "All right then. Mount up. Let's go crash this party and find your parents."

CHAPTER TWENTY-ONE

M ad Dog rode around the corner to Tredegar. The spotlights in the sky seemed to announce their arrival. Sam figured Mad Dog would drop them off at the curb and ride off to do whatever it is that bikers do at night—maybe head back to their hideout at the hydro plant on Belle Isle. Instead, they pulled into the parking lot, engines roaring, and circled a big ice sculpture next to the main tent.

Everyone at the gala stopped what they were doing to look up at the menacing motorbikes. After three circles around the lot, the bikes pulled to a stop, lined up in a row, and killed their engines. A man walked out of the crowd toward the motorcycles, hands waving like he was shooing flies away the food tables. "Excuse me, gentlemen, this is a private event. Please move along." It was Professor Evanshade.

Sam, Derek, and Caitlin slid off the bikes and pulled off their helmets. The professor's face brightened with surprise when he recognized them. "Oh my golly! What are you kids doing on these motorcycles?"

Sam stepped forward. "We, uh, got a ride from some new …" he paused, trying to think of the right word to describe Mad Dog and his crew, "friends."

Mad Dog pulled off his helmet, stepping off his bike. "Luke DeWitt," he said, extending his hand to the professor for a shake.

"Well," the professor stammered, "isn't this a surprise. Very nice to meet you, Mr. DeWitt. I see that we have some mutual friends."

Mad Dog grinned with a nod. "Yeah, but we'd best be heading out. Enjoy the party, kids." He reached out and gave Sam a fist bump. "Let me know if you have any more trouble."

"Okay, we will," answered Sam.

"And thanks!" said Derek.

"Let's roll, boys," Mad Dog called to his buddies, the bikes roaring back to life. He eased away from the professor and the kids, turning with a wave of his hand. Soon the red taillights of the bikes blended into the haze of the spotlights.

Sam stood for a moment, listening as the three motors revved down the lane, gradually fading into the sounds of the night. He glanced past Professor Evanshade and saw Mom and Dad and Caitlin's parents walking toward them. He swallowed hard and looked over at Derek. This wasn't going to be good. Where was Meghan and her careless attitude when they needed her?

"Boys," said Dad, peering down at them, his single word packed with meaning.

"Hi, Dad," answered Sam, meekly attempting a smile.

Derek tried a different approach. "Mom, Dad, I'd really like to hear more about your trip to Paris!" He put his arm around Mom's shoulder and tried to lead her into the party.

"Not so fast, buster," she answered.

"I don't remember you asking to ride on any motor-cycles," said Dad. "Did I miss something?"

Caitlin walked up to her parents, Mrs. Murphy looking her over to make sure she wasn't hurt. Sam couldn't hear what she was saying, but she kept glancing back over at Sam and Derek as if she was second-guessing her daughter's choice of friends.

"I'm sorry, Dad, but it was completely unexpected," Derek tried to explain. "We ran into Cameron and Sean, and they almost threw us in the river to kill us, and then they made me go across the bridge to get his hat, but they really had it the whole time, and then I got captured by the Confederate Ghosts …"

"Ghosts?" Mom interrupted.

"Yeah, the Confederate Ghosts," said Sam.

"They're the bikers," said Caitlin, stepping closer and nodding her head.

"So they kidnapped me in the hydro plant but Sam and Caitlin rescued me until we ran into Mad Dog ..." Derek took a deep breath from speaking so fast.

"Mad Dog?" asked Mr. Murphy.

"That was him talking to the professor," said Caitlin. "That's not his real name. It's really Luke."

"Oh, well as long as it isn't his real name ..." said Mrs. Murphy.

"So then," continued Derek, "he turned out to be nice, and they gave us a ride back across the bridge on their motorcycles, until we ran into Cameron. Mad Dog scared him and told him to stop bullying us."

"Cameron Talley? When has he been bullying you?"

"Don't worry about it, Mom," said Sam. "It's been taken care of."

"I don't like the sound of that," Mom answered.

"I don't like the sound of any of this," added Dad, shaking his head. "We're going to have a long talk about this after your mother and I get a good night's sleep. I can only imagine what you two have been up to with Meghan this week if this is what happens when we're back." He let out a long sigh, shaking his head some more, like he was feeling older by the second.

"I still don't think I even understand what happened," said Mom.

"Maybe it's best that we keep it that way, Mom," said Derek.

"Don't bet on it," said Dad.

Professor Evanshade moved over to them. "I don't mean to interrupt, but we're about to close our evening with the firing of a cannon. Would the kids like to assist lighting the fuse?" He looked up at the two sets of parents for approval.

Sam's dad closed his eyes and nodded. Thankfully, he seemed too tired to argue.

"Yes! Thanks, Dad," exclaimed Derek.

"Just stay where we can see you," said Caitlin's dad, also nodding.

"Thanks, Daddy!" Caitlin rushed over to join the boys and the professor next to one of the old cannons under a spotlight.

Another man helped stuff some powder into the cannon with a long stick with a pad on the end of it. "Stand over here, children." He pointed to a rope sticking out of the back of the cannon.

"Is this really gonna fire?" asked Derek.

"Shouldn't we aim it away from the parking lot?" asked Sam. He pictured a giant cannonball flying through the air and blowing up their minivan. That would be spectacular, but it would probably send Dad over the edge. Plus, they wouldn't have a way home.

The professor chuckled. "It *is* a real cannon, but we won't be loading any ammunition tonight. There's no lead ball, just powder."

Sam let out a deep breath, happy that the minivan would be spared.

"But," the professor continued, "it does pack quite a bang, so you might want to cover your ears since we're so close." He bent down, picked up a thin stick, and flicked it on the brick walkway. The stick was a long match that suddenly burst into a flame. He turned to Caitlin. "Young lady, would you please do us the honor of lighting the cannon?"

"Aww," moaned Derek.

"Sorry, Derek, ladies first. Why don't you boys count us down from three?" Professor Evanshade looked up at the crowd. "Move back, ladies and gentlemen, and cover your ears!"

"Three ... two ... one!" counted Sam and Derek in unison.

Caitlin touched the flame to the end of the rope, which immediately sizzled. The flame zipped along the fabric to the cannon and the powder.

Sam leaned over, his hands muffling his ears. He braced himself for the blast as the flame met the metal of the cannon. Just when it seemed like nothing was going to happen—BOOM!

The ground seemed to shake as the cannon exploded.

"Wow!" hollered Derek. "That was awesome."

"Pretty incredible, isn't it?" agreed Professor Evanshade. "Can you imagine being here the night that General Lee's troops evacuated the city? Richmond was in flames, and the munitions here at Tredegar began exploding something terrible. It must have been quite a time."

"I think I would lose my hearing," said Caitlin, laughing.

Sam looked toward where the Lincoln statue sat behind the building. He pictured the president walking through the streets of the city the morning after everything had burned and exploded. He wondered what would have been going through the mind of the tall man with the beard.

"You kids still have your hearing?" called Mom, walking over with Dad to the cannon. "That was quite an explosion."

"What?" yelled Derek, pretending that his eardrums had burst.

"Pretty cool, huh, Mom?" said Sam.

"I think it's time we headed out, boys. It's late," said Dad.

"What time is it right now in Paris?" asked Caitlin.

Dad looked at his watch. "Let's see, it's six hours ahead, so it would be four in the morning."

"No wonder I'm tired," yawned Mom.

Mr. and Mrs. Murphy walked up too. "Thank the professor for the invite, Caitlin, so we can go."

"Thanks, Professor Evanshade," called Caitlin.

"Yeah, thanks," added Derek.

"You're very welcome, kids," the professor answered. "It always seems to be exciting whenever I see you, and this was no exception."

As Sam reached his minivan, he realized how tired he was. So much had happened that evening.

Caitlin turned and hugged him. "I'm glad things turned out the way they did. I was a little nervous there for a while."

Sam chuckled. "A little? I could hardly breathe!"

Caitlin smiled. "Maybe the rest of the summer can stay a little quieter. What do you think?"

Sam nodded, looking over at his parents. He knew they'd be keeping a tighter watch over him now that they were back from their trip. Things would be quieter whether he wanted them to be or not.

He'd probably get stuck hanging out with Mr. Haskins the rest of the summer. At least now they could compare ghost stories. He wondered if Mr. Haskins would believe that he rode on Mad Dog DeWitt's motorcycle. Probably not. Sam could hardly believe it himself.

"See you at the bookstore next Tuesday afternoon?" said Caitlin.

"Sounds good." Sam waved and followed Derek into the minivan.

As they pulled away, he took one more peek across the water to Belle Isle. A flash of light caught his eye in the distance, streaking over the water like a comet. "Whoa, Derek, look at that!"

"What is it?"

"A light. I saw it over the rapids." He stared back across the water, resting his head against the seat, his eyes suddenly feeling heavy. "It was the ghosts," he mumbled softly.

"Sure, Sam," said Derek.

Sam wondered if he'd really seen something, or if his imagination was just getting the best of him. Maybe it was Mad Dog heading back to the hydro plant for a mean game of cards, or Lee's ghost preparing for one more stand in his capital city, or a Union soldier still trying to escape. Or maybe, just maybe, President Lincoln was making one last visit to Richmond, pushing up the James with his son Tad, unaware that his life was only days from ending. Perhaps he was hoping to catch one more glimpse of the southern city where, even a hundred and fifty years later, the effects of the war were still smoldering in time.

SECRET OF THE STAIRCASE

THE VIRGINIA MYSTERIES BOOK 4

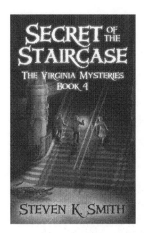

Something's lurking beneath the famous staircase at The
Jefferson, Richmond's historic downtown hotel. Back in 1895,
when the hotel opened, real alligators roamed free in the
courtyard fountains. That was ages ago ... or was it? When
young brothers Sam and Derek arrive at The Jefferson for an
elegant wedding weekend with their parents, they love
exploring the old hotel. But when the wedding rings go
missing and Sam is blamed, the boys and their friends must
hunt down the truth no matter where it leads. If they're not
careful, they might become dinner for the hotel's most
unusual guests.

ACKNOWLEDGMENTS

I couldn't do any of this without the love, grace, and inspiration I receive from my family. Thank you to my wife, Mary, and my three boys, Matthew, Josh, and Aaron, for cheering me on.

Thank you also to so many friends and family who have supported my efforts and provided enthusiasm and encouragement - Alicia, Ryan, Mom, Dad, Robin, Jean, Ray, Ali, and Julie. All my friends at Bettie Weaver Elementary, CHAT, St. John's Church Foundation, Colonial Williamsburg, Bella Arte Gallery, and James River Writers. Thanks also to my favorite writing podcasts, which provide invaluable resources to me and indie writers everywhere: the Creative Penn Podcast, Self Publishing Podcast, and Rocking Self Publishing Podcast, for hours of inspiration and ideas while driving and flying. Thanks to my editor, Kim Sheard at Another View

Editing, and Dane at Ebook Launch for designing all the great new covers for The Virginia Mysteries series.

I really never imagined I'd be writing books, but it's been an amazing time. Thank you to all my readers, young and old(er), who have joined me on this journey. Keep dreaming big and pushing toward your goals. You never know what adventure you might stumble upon along the way.

ALSO BY STEVEN K. SMITH

The Virginia Mysteries:

Summer of the Woods
Mystery on Church Hill
Ghosts of Belle Isle
Secret of the Staircase
Midnight at the Mansion
Shadows at Jamestown
Spies at Mount Vernon
Escape from Monticello
Pictures at the Protest
Pirates on the Bay

Brother Wars Series:

Brother Wars
Cabin Eleven
The Big Apple

Final Kingdom Trilogy (Ages 10+)

The Missing
The Recruit
The Bridge

ABOUT THE AUTHOR

Steven K. Smith is the author of *The Virginia Mysteries*, *Brother Wars*, and *Final Kingdom* series for middle grade readers. He lives with his wife, three sons, and a golden retriever in Richmond, Virginia.

For more information, visit:

www.stevenksmith.net

Email: steve@myboys3.com

Facebook & Instagram: @stevenksmithauthor

Twitter: @stevenksmith1

CHAT

Sam, Derek, and Caitlin aren't the only kids who crave adventure. Whether near woods in the country or amidst tall buildings and the busy urban streets of a city, every child needs exciting ways to explore his or her imagination, excel at learning and have fun.

A portion of the proceeds from *The Virginia Mysteries* series will be donated to the great work of **CHAT (Church Hill Activities & Tutoring)**. CHAT is a non-profit group that works with kids in the Church Hill neighborhood of inner-city Richmond, Virginia.

To learn more about CHAT, including opportunities to volunteer or contribute financially, visit **www. chatrichmond.org.**

DID YOU ENJOY GHOSTS OF BELLE ISLE?

WOULD YOU ... REVIEW?

Online reviews are crucial for indie authors like me. They help bring credibility and make books more discoverable by new readers. No matter where you purchased your book, if you could take a few moments and give an honest review at **Amazon** or **Goodreads**, I'd be grateful.

If you're a teacher, be sure to check out the reading comprehension quiz, in-person and virtual classroom visit opportunities, historical links, and other materials on my website at stevenksmith.net.

Made in the USA
Columbia, SC
14 November 2021